D0498671

The Jake Drake Collection

Andrew Clements

The Jake Drake Collection

Bully Buster

Know-It-All

Class Clown

Cover illustration by Marla Frazee
Interior illustrations by Janet Pedersen

ATHENEUM BOOKS FOR YOUNG READERS
New York London Toronto Sydney New Delhi

Atheneum Books for Young Readers
An imprint of Simon & Schuster Children's Publishing Division
1230 Avenue of the Americas, New York, NY 10020
Bully Buster copyright © 2001 by Andrew Clements
Know-It-All copyright © 2001 by Andrew Clements
Class Clown copyright © 2002 by Andrew Clements
Cover illustrations copyright © 2007 by Marla Frazee
Interior illustrations copyright © 2007 by Janet Pedersen
All rights reserved, including the right of reproduction
in whole or in part in any form.
Atheneum Books for Young Readers is a registered trademark
of Simon & Schuster, Inc.
For information about special discounts for bulk purchases,
please contact Simon & Schuster Special Sales at 1-866-506-1949
or business@simonandschuster.com.
The Simon & Schuster Speakers Bureau can bring authors to
your live event. For more information or to book an event contact the
Simon & Schuster Speakers Bureau at 1-866-248-3049 or visit our
website at www.simonspeakers.com.
The illustrations for this book were rendered in pen and ink.
Manufactured in the United States of America 0712 FFG
2 4 6 8 10 9 7 5 3 1
ISBN 978-1-4424-8180-0

Jake Drake

BULLY BUSTER

**To Kathy, Mary, and Frank Despres
in appreciation of their loving, dedicated service
to the children of Westborough**

Contents

CHAPTER ONE   Bully-Magnet   1

CHAPTER TWO   SuperBully   11

CHAPTER THREE   From Bad to Worse   18

CHAPTER FOUR   Bullyitis   23

CHAPTER FIVE   What Abby Said   28

CHAPTER SIX   Playing It Cool   33

CHAPTER SEVEN   Learning My Lesson   39

CHAPTER EIGHT   Dangerous Duo   44

CHAPTER NINE   Surprises and Questions   51

CHAPTER TEN   Busted Link   61

CHAPTER ONE

Bully-Magnet

I'm Jake—Jake Drake. I'm in fourth grade. Which is my best grade so far. I've got a man teacher this year, Mr. Thompson. He's pretty old, but he's not mean. And he likes the same kinds of books I do. Adventure stories, books about volcanoes and jungles and the ocean, joke books, Calvin and Hobbes—stuff like that.

But there is one thing about Mr. Thompson that's weird. Pete was the first to see it. Which makes sense. Pete is a science kid. He collects bugs and fossils and plants, and he knows all their names, and he's maybe the smartest kid in the school.

After about two weeks of school, Pete pointed at Mr. Thompson. Then he whispered, "He's wearing those pants again."

"Which pants?" I said.

"*Those* pants," Pete said. "The same pants he wore yesterday and the day before and the day before that. I think he wears the same pants *every* day."

"No way," I said. "He probably has a lot of pants that are the same, that's all."

So Pete said, "I'm going to test my theory."

See what I mean? That's how science kids are.

That afternoon we had read-aloud time on the rug, and Mr. Thompson sat in a beanbag chair. Pete sat right next to Mr. Thompson and a little behind him. Mr. Thompson started reading, and he got to the part when the Swiss Family Robinson wrecks their ship.

All the other kids were looking at Mr. Thompson's face or at the ceiling or somewhere. I was watching Pete.

Pete pulled his hand out of his pocket. His

hand went behind Mr. Thompson's foot, just for a second, and then back to his pocket. And then Pete sat and listened like everyone else.

When reading was over, I got next to Pete and whispered, "What did you do?"

Pete grinned and pulled something out of his pocket. It was a little black marker, the kind that doesn't wash out.

I got behind Mr. Thompson and looked down. On the right leg of his pants, on the back of his cuff, was a tiny black spot.

So that's how we found out that Mr. Thompson really has two pairs of pants. Every Thursday he wears tan pants that are just like the other pair, but they don't have the little black spot and they look a little newer. Pete's theory is that Thursday must be laundry day at Mr. Thompson's house. Because every Friday, we can see the little spot again.

My best friend is Phil Willis. Everyone calls him Willie. Willie isn't in my class this year. We have gym class and music class and art class together, but for the rest of the time Willie has Mrs. Steele.

I'm glad I have Mr. Thompson. I mean, Mrs. Steele is okay, but Willie has a lot more homework than I do. Also, Mrs. Steele is a spelling nut. And a math nut. And a social studies nut. I guess she's a nut about everything. That's why Willie's favorite class this year is gym.

Like I said, I'm in fourth grade. That means I've been going to school for five years now. And if you count the two years I went to Miss Lulu's Dainty Diaper Day Care Center, plus one year of preschool, then it's more like eight years. Eight years of school.

So here's what I can't figure out. If everybody who works at school is so smart, how come they can't get rid of the bullies? How come when it comes to bullies, kids are mostly on their own?

Because every year, it's the same thing. Bullies.

Here's what I mean. Okay, it was way back when I was three. I was at Miss Lulu's Day Care. It was the middle of the morning on my second day, and I was standing in line for milk and cookies. And this kid with a runny nose and baggy overalls cut right in front of me.

I didn't say anything because I didn't know any better. Remember, I was only three back then. For all I knew, kids with runny noses got to go first.

So I took my cookies and my milk and sat down at a table. Nose Boy sat down across from me. I smiled at him and took a drink of my milk.

And what did he do? He reached over and grabbed both my cookies. Before I could swallow my milk, he took a big slobbery bite from each one. Then he put them back on my napkin. And then he smiled at me.

I looked at the stuff coming out of his nose. Then I looked at my cookies. And then I turned my head to look for Miss Lulu.

She was still handing out goodies. A crime had taken place, but Miss Lulu was busy.

So I reached over real fast and took *his* cookies. But then I looked down. Nose Boy had already taken a bite out of them, too.

He smiled again, and I could see the crumbs and chocolate chips stuck in his teeth. So I thought to myself, *Who needs a snack anyway?* I slid his cookies back across the table, drank the rest of my milk, and went outside to play.

Three minutes later I was on a swing, just trying to get it going. And somebody grabbed the chain. That's right—it was Nose Boy again.

He snuffled a little and said, "Mine." Nose Boy wasn't much of a talker.

Then I said something like, "I got here first." That was a mistake. The first rule of dealing with a bully is: Never try to tell him why he's wrong. Bullies don't like that.

He yanked hard on the chain and said, "No! Mine!"

I looked around, and Miss Lulu was on the other side of the playground. Then Nose Boy jerked on the chain again, so I got off the swing.

Nose Boy was my first bully. And for the next four years, I was a bully-magnet.

In preschool it was Mike Rada. I called him Destructo. Blocks, LEGOs, Popsicle sticks, crayons, and paper—no matter what I made or what it was made out of, Destructo tore it to bits.

In kindergarten it was Kenny Russell. Kenny

was King Bump. There are a lot of times every day when a bump or a shove can be bad. Like if you're standing next to a puddle at the bus stop. Or when you're drinking a carton of chocolate milk, or maybe when you're working on a painting. If there was a bumpable moment, King Bump was there, all through kindergarten.

In first grade my main bully was Jack Lerner, also known as The Fist. Jack never actually hit me. He just hit things close to me. Like my lunch bag. Like every day. A big fist does a very bad thing to a Wonder Bread sandwich. And I learned real fast not to bring any little containers of pudding. All during first grade I ate cookie crumbs for dessert.

So that was me. I was Jake Drake, the bully-magnet. It was like all the bullies got together to choose their favorite target. Every bully for miles around seemed to know that I was the perfect kid to pick on. And I think I finally figured out why they all liked me so much.

For one thing, bullies need a kid who's just the right size. If the kid is too big, then there

might be a fight someday. Bullies don't like to fight. And if the kid is too small, then the bullying is too easy. There's no challenge.

Another thing about me that bullies like is that I don't have a big brother, or even a big sister. I just have Abby, and she's two years younger than me. Bullies figure out stuff like that right away.

And bullies can tell that I'm not the kind of kid who runs to tell the teacher all my problems. Whiny tattletales make bad bully-bait.

Also, I think I look kind of brainy. Most bullies don't seem so smart, and when they see a kid who looks like he is, something inside a bully says, "Oh, yeah? Well, now you've got to deal with *me*, smart guy!"

And I guess I am a smart guy, because I *am* good at thinking. And because I'm a good thinker, I finally learned what to do about bullies. But I didn't figure all this out at once. It took me four long years. It took having to deal with Nose Boy, and then Destructo, and King Bump, and The Fist.

It also took being picked on by a Certified, Grade A, SuperBully. Which is what happened back when I was in second grade. That's the year I became Jake Drake, Bully Buster.

CHAPTER TWO

SuperBully

Second grade started out great. My mom and dad had asked for me to be in Mrs. Brattle's class. They told me she was the best teacher at Despres Elementary School. She smiled a lot, and there wasn't any homework, and there was a lot of neat stuff all over her room, so I was happy she was my teacher.

Phil Willis had Mrs. Brattle, too. Willie and I were already best friends back in second grade, and we had fun every day. We sat at the same group of tables. We were reading partners. We ate lunch together every day, and we always goofed around during recess. We didn't ride the same bus, but after school sometimes I went to his house, and sometimes he came over to mine.

Best of all, Mrs. Brattle's class had zero bullies. Not one. It was great. I still had to be careful at lunchtime and out on the playground, but most of the time my life was bully-free.

Then, right before Halloween, a new kid moved to town. The minute he walked into Mrs. Brattle's room, I knew I was in trouble.

Mrs. Brattle said, "Class, we have a new student today. His name is Link Baxter."

She kept talking, and we all looked at the new kid. I could see he was kind of tall for a second grader. He had brown hair and a pointy nose and long arms with big hands.

Link Baxter stood there and started looking around the room at all of us, too. When he came to me, he stopped. I looked into his face and I saw that Link Baxter had beady little eyes—bully-eyes. And Link saw me seeing this. And then he smiled at me.

It was not a nice smile.

Then Mrs. Brattle, this lady who was supposed to be such a great teacher, what did she do? She put Link at the same group of desks with me and Willie.

Right away Willie whispered, "Hi. I'm Phil, but really I'm Willie. That's my nickname."

You see, Willie has never had any trouble with bullies, mostly because he's too small. He's a nice kid and he minds his own business, and bullies don't even seem to notice him.

So Link smiled at Willie and said, "Hi."

Then Willie pointed at me and said, "This is Jake."

Link Baxter pointed his beady eyes at me and smiled that bully-smile again. And he said, "Jake. Okay."

I tried to smile and nod at him, but I know I looked kind of spooked, because I *was* spooked. And Link could see I was spooked. And he liked it. And that's when I knew I was in big bully-trouble.

Link was only eight years old, just like me. But I could tell right from the start that Link had big plans. He wanted to be the MVP on the Bully

All-Star team. He wanted to make it into the Bullies Hall of Fame. And me, Jake Drake, *I* was his new project.

On that first day when Link came to my class, we practiced handwriting. Mrs. Brattle passed out some lined white paper. We had to write six sentences very, very neatly. Handwriting practice was the only time we could use a pen instead of a pencil.

I loved using my pen. It was made of bright red plastic, and it had black ink. There was a little button on the side. When I pushed the button, the pen went *click*, and the top popped up.

So I was in the middle of my fifth sentence, almost done. The pen was gliding over the smooth paper. My handwriting looked great.

Then Link gave his desk a quick shake. My desk was touching his desk, so my pen went jerking all over. My paper was a mess.

I looked over at Link, and he smiled. Then he whispered, "Nice pen."

So I went up to Mrs. Brattle and got a new piece of paper. I started copying my sentences

again. But now I watched Link all the time to be sure he didn't shake his desk again. I was so nervous that I messed up two more pieces of paper all by myself. And Link didn't make a move.

So I settled down. I was on the very last sentence. Mrs. Brattle was helping a kid at the back of the room. So Link reached over real fast and flicked my ear. Not hard, just enough to make me jump. My pen skidded, and my paper was a mess all over again.

You see, Link was no ordinary bully. Any big kid can push a little kid around. That's one kind of bullying. But this was different. Link Baxter, well . . . he got inside my head—and it only took him twenty minutes. No doubt about it. This was a bully with real talent.

So there I was, asking Mrs. Brattle for my fifth piece of paper, and she said, "Jake, you should be more careful."

And I almost shouted, "Yeah, well, *you* should pay more attention. Don't you know there's a SuperBully loose in your classroom?"

But of course I didn't say that. Because the

second rule about bullies is that if you tattle to the teacher, things might get a lot worse. And I had a feeling things were going to be bad enough already.

And I was right.

CHAPTER THREE

From Bad to Worse

So I got on the bus after Link's first day of school. I looked out the window. I saw Link walking behind Mrs. Brattle. She was showing him which bus to ride home.

"Please," I whispered. "Not my bus. Not bus three. Please, please, please, not bus three."

But Mrs. Brattle led him right over to bus number three. And ten seconds later, Link was on my bus, standing there next to me. Looking down at me.

In a voice much louder than it needed to be,

he said, "Hey, Fake, anyone else gonna sit here?"

I looked up and I remembered how tall he was. But now he was messing with my name. And he already had me mad and scared at the same time. But I didn't care, because I didn't want him to make fun of my name.

So I said, "My name's Jake, Jake Drake." And right away I knew I had made a mistake. Because now he knew that I cared about him goofing around with my name.

Link smiled that special bully-smile. He said, "Yeah, I know. Like I said. Your name's Fake, Fake Drake." And that made the other kids on the bus start laughing. And then he sat down next to me.

He didn't push me or hit me, because any-body can do that sort of thing. He was a new kind of bully. He was a SuperBully.

I felt my ears turning red. My lips were clamped together. I turned my head away from him and looked out the window. I was ready for the next attack.

But it didn't come. A fourth grader in the seat across had a baseball glove. So Link said, "What's the best Little League team in this town?"

And Link started talking about how he was on the top team in his old town. He didn't want to join a new team unless it was going to be a winner.

It was like I wasn't there. I was right there on the seat next to him, but I might as well have been on the moon.

The bus stopped at Maple Street, and some kids got off. Then at Cross Street, and more kids got off. And then the bus was at my stop, Greenwood Street.

So I said, "I have to get off at this stop." About ten kids stood up as the bus slowed down. But Link kept on talking to the fourth grader about Little League.

So I said it louder. "This is my stop. I have to get off here."

I looked over the seat in front of me. There were only three kids left, up by the bus driver.

So I shouted, "NOW. I have to get off NOW!"

The bus driver looked up into her mirror and frowned. But Link smiled at her. And loud enough for everyone to hear, he said, "Oops.

Almost forgot, Fake. I'm a new kid, remember? This is my stop, too. This is where me and Fake Drake get off the bus."

Following Link Baxter off the bus? That was one of the worst moments of my life. As I went down those tall black steps, I thought, *Every morning and every afternoon and all day long for the rest of second grade—maybe even for the rest of my life—it's going to be me and Link Baxter.*

Something was going to have to change.

CHAPTER FOUR

Bullyitis

Link didn't even talk to me when I got off the bus. He just walked away. I watched him. He crossed Greenwood Street and started to walk down Park Street.

And then I remembered. Of course! Link had moved into the Carsons' old house. The house had been for sale, and now it was Link's house. Right on Park Street. Right around the corner from me.

When I walked into my house, I didn't even

say hi to my mom. I dropped my book bag on the floor. Then I went right to the playroom.

My little sister, Abby, was watching a puppet show on TV. It was her favorite show.

I said, "Give me that!" And I grabbed the remote from her. She frowned at me and stuck her tongue out. Then I changed the channel to *Batman*.

Abby said, "Hey! I'm watching my puppets."

And I said, "Oh, yeah?" And I went over to her. She was sitting on a big pillow on the floor. I felt a lot taller than Abby. I said, "Well, I'm watching *Batman*, and you can't stop me." Then I kicked her pillow.

Abby yelled, "Ow! Ow! That hurt! Mom, Jake stole the remote. And he just kicked me, HARD!"

Mom came in. She was walking her fast walk. That's her "You're in big trouble" walk.

She stopped and stood over me. She said, "Jake Drake, you know better than to come in here and make a fuss! You come right back to the kitchen and pick up your book bag. And give that remote back to your sister."

I tossed the remote to Abby. By mistake it hit her on the knee. "OWWW!" Now she really yelled, and she tried to cry a little too.

So real quick, I said, "Sorry." But I was too late. Mom took me by the arm and marched me to the kitchen.

She put me on a chair. Then she said, "Jake, we do not treat others like that in this family, and you know it! What's gotten into you!?"

And then it hit me. It was Link. Link had gotten into me! I was being like Link. I had caught BULLYITIS!

But I couldn't tell my mom about Link. Because my mom might call Link's mom. Then Link would tell every kid on the bus how Fake Drake went and cried to his mommy. And every day on the bus for the rest of my life I would hear about how I'm such a big baby.

So I said, "Sorry, Mom." Then I gave a big sigh. "I guess I'm just tired and hungry."

Moms love to hear that. Tired and hungry— that's stuff that moms know how to fix.

Mom patted me on the head. Then she fixed me a peanut butter sandwich and a glass of milk.

And she said, "I'll make sure you get to bed early tonight, sweetheart. But when that sandwich is gone, you have to go apologize to Abby."

So I ate slowly. But then I put my dish and my glass in the sink and went to look for Abby.

And I thought it was going to be like all the other times I had told Abby I was sorry.

But it wasn't.

CHAPTER FIVE

What Abby Said

Abby was only in kindergarten back then—back when I was in second grade. Even so, Abby wasn't stupid like a lot of little kids are.

I'd never tell her this, but Abby's okay to talk to sometimes. You know, for a sister. I mean, since I don't have a dog or anything. Abby's kind of like a pet who can talk. Sort of like a parrot, I guess.

Anyway, I told Abby I was sorry.

"It's okay," she said.

See what I mean? How Abby's kind of like a

pet? You know how if you yell at a dog, it gets all scared of you, or maybe mad? But then you pat it on the head, and it starts wagging its tail again? That's the way Abby is.

She was still watching the puppets. They were painting some clouds on a wall. Really dumb.

Then I told Abby about Link.

And Abby said, "His sister came to school today. Linda Baxter. She's in kindergarten with me. She's a bully, too."

I said, "Really?"

"Yes," said Abby. "Linda took Sara's crayons. I saw."

Abby started moving her arms like the puppets.

I said, "So she took Sara's crayons?"

Abby nodded, only half listening. "Yes. The best colors. Linda said, 'If you tell, I'll break them.' At snack time Sara gave Linda a Ritz cracker. Then Linda let Sara use the yellow crayon."

So there it was. The Case of the Kidnapped Crayons.

And I said to myself, *Linda Baxter is only in* kindergarten! *Link's baby sister is already a SuperBully.* And then I thought, *Imagine what*

her big brother is going to do to me!

Not a good thought.

Abby kept watching the puppets. The show was almost over. The puppets were starting to sing. It's the part of the show that almost makes me throw up.

Then I remembered something. I remembered going to visit Gramma and Grampa in Florida. It was just me and Abby. And I was mad because I always had to do everything with Abby. She was just four. She was still in nursery school, and I was already a big first grader. I hated hanging around with such a baby. I was mean to Abby the whole time.

So I said, "Remember how I was mean to you when we went to Florida?"

Abby was nodding to the music. But she said, "I remember."

And I said, "How come you didn't get mad at me?"

Abby shrugged. "If I get mad, I feel mean. I don't like to feel mean. So I don't get mad."

Then Abby started to sing along with the puppets. I did not want to throw up, so I went to my room. I flopped onto my bed so I could think about my problems.

Part of me wished I could get a ride to school with Dad every morning. Then I wouldn't have to ride the bus with Link. And maybe I could go to the library for recess. And then Mom could pick me up after school.

Part of me wished I would grow ten inches in one night. Then tomorrow morning I would get on the bus. I would sit next to Link. I would push his face against the window. I would paint his nose with a red Magic Marker. I would call him Fink. Fink Baxter.

But I kept thinking. And Abby was right. It's not fun to feel mean. Link acted like it *was* fun. But it wasn't, really—was it? No. It couldn't be.

As I went to sleep that night, here's what I said to myself: *Tomorrow, I will not get mad at Link. No matter what. Then he will see that it's not fun to be mean.*

It worked for Abby and me.

But would it work for a SuperBully?

CHAPTER SIX

Playing It Cool

In the morning, Link made sure that he sat next to me on the bus. First thing, he wiped mud from his shoes onto my book bag. But I just smiled and brushed it off. Very cool.

He called me Jake Flake. I laughed and said, "Yeah, that's a good one! Or how about Snake Drake? Or . . . Cheesecake Drake? Or maybe . . . maybe, Shaky Jake? Yeah, Shaky Jake."

Everybody on the bus laughed. But it was me making them laugh, not Link. I was playing it cool.

Link didn't like it. His beady little eyes got meaner and meaner. And when we got to school, he pushed his way up to the front so he got off the bus first. He even pushed some fifth graders.

In class it got worse. Link stuck some gum onto my math workbook. I just smiled and put a piece of paper over the sticky part. I kept working, cool as could be.

During art class Link poured some gold glitter into the paint I was using. I said, "Nice idea!" And I kept painting.

Later, the art teacher said, "Jake, I *love* what you've done there. Very creative."

Very creative, and very *cool.*

I was worried about recess. The playground is big. Anything can happen out there.

Sure enough, Link cut in line and got behind me on the sliding board. I slid down, and he came down behind me really fast. He tried to bump me into a puddle. But I stepped aside real fast, and his foot went into some mud.

It's a good thing Mrs. Brattle was standing so close. Otherwise, Link might have tried to make me lick that mud off his shoe or something.

After lunch I was in the boys' room washing my hands. I looked in the mirror, and there was Link. Smiling. I tried to smile back, but it was hard. I was scared.

Link kept smiling. He started to wash his hands at the sink next to me. And when I got a paper towel, he cupped his hands and threw a ton of water right at me. Right down the front of my tan pants. A big brown wet spot.

Then in this baby voice Link said, "Wook, wook! Wittle Jakey had a accident!" A bunch of fourth graders started pointing and laughing.

I tried to laugh, too. I tried to be cool, but I couldn't. I couldn't laugh. Not about that. I got angry. I felt like flames were going to shoot out of my eyes.

And Link saw. He saw me get mad. Then he saw me get even madder about him seeing me get mad. And Link's beady little eyes and his smirky little mouth laughed. At me.

I stayed in the boys' room as long as I could. I rubbed on my pants with paper towels. I fanned my pants with my hands. But when I went back to class, there was still a big dark spot.

And Link had been whispering. Everybody looked at me when I came in the door. My face turned bright pink. And when I sat down across from Link, he held his nose and made a face.

I couldn't help it. I was so mad. And it made me feel mean. And I lost it. I turned toward Link and I punched him on the shoulder with all my might.

Might is something I don't have a lot of. So I know I didn't really hurt him.

But Link was a lot better at acting than Abby. He grabbed his shoulder and knocked a book off his desk.

"Ahh!" he shouted. "Ahh! My arm, my arm!"

Mrs. Brattle was there in one second flat. "Jake! I am *ashamed* of you!"

Link let his arm flop down like it was broken. He whimpered, "Ahh, my arm, my arm! It hurts."

Mrs. Brattle said, "Ted, please help Link down to the nurse's office. And Jake, you come with me."

As Link left the room, he peeked a look back at me. And he smiled.

Link Baxter was off to get some ice and some friendly words from the nurse.

And me? I was off to talk with the principal—probably not a happy little chat. And my pants still had a big stain down the front.

Mrs. Brattle walked me down the hall. On the way, I figured something out. Link was a bigger problem than Abby had ever faced.

This was war, and I was losing. Big time.

Not cool. Not cool at all.

CHAPTER SEVEN

Learning My Lesson

When people are mad at you, they do a lot of pointing. In the office, Mrs. Brattle pointed to a chair. She said, "Wait here." No smiles. Then she went into the principal's office.

A minute later she came out, and so did Mrs. Karp. Mrs. Karp pointed to her office and said, "In there, Jake."

I had never been to the principal's office before. There was a big gray desk. There was a row of big gray bookcases. And there was a big gray principal. Mrs. Karp had gray shoes, a gray

dress, and gray hair. And she was taller than Mrs. Brattle. Even taller than my dad.

She pointed at a gray chair in front of her desk. "Sit there, Jake." So I sat down. Then she said, "You know it's against the rules to hit someone, don't you." It wasn't a question.

And I said, "Yes, I know."

"Then why did you hit Link Baxter?"

This was the tricky part. If I told about Link being a bully, then I would be a tattletale. But if I didn't say *something*, then she would think I was some crazy hitter. So I pointed at the spot on my pants. And I said, "Some water got on my pants in the boys' room. And I thought Link was making fun."

So simple. So true. So easy for Mrs. Karp to understand. And she did. Just like that. She got a friendly look on her face and said, "I understand about feeling embarrassed, Jake. But do you see that hitting is wrong, no matter what?"

And I said, "Yes." Because it was true. I really was sorry I had hit Link. I did not want to have a fight with Link. Ever. For two reasons.

First, because it's not good to hit and kick

and scratch and pull hair and roll around on the ground. And second, because I knew what would happen to me if I ever *did* get in a fight with Link. I would turn into one huge purple bruise.

So Mrs. Karp sent me back to my classroom. She didn't even call my mom.

As she opened the door to her office for me she said, "I'm sure you've learned your lesson, haven't you, Jake?"

And I said, "Yes, Mrs. Karp." Only I didn't know if we were talking about the same lesson.

As I walked from the school office toward Mrs. Brattle's room, Link came out of the nurse's office. I think he had been waiting for me. He walked beside me. In the empty hallway Link seemed bigger than ever.

He gave me that bully-smile and said, "Nice move, Flake. Have a good time with the principal?"

This was the first time I had been alone with Link. I was scared, but I said, "It wasn't so bad." We kept walking.

Being alone with Link was different. And I thought that maybe a bully stops being a bully if there aren't some other kids around to watch. I thought that maybe he's only a SuperBully when he has an audience. For a second, it felt like Link Baxter was just this big kid, and I was walking down the hall with him.

Back then I didn't know as much about bullies as I do now. So I said, "How come you pick on me?"

Wrong question. The SuperBully was back. Link looked at me like I was a bug. He said, "Dumb question." And I thought maybe he was going to push me into a locker or something.

But he didn't. And we just kept walking.

But it was like my question confused him. And just before we got back to room twenty-three, I knew. I knew why he didn't answer the question.

He didn't because he *couldn't*. He couldn't tell me why because he didn't really know.

But there had to be a reason why Link was a bully.

And if I could figure out that reason—or if I could give him a reason NOT to be a bully—then Link Baxter, SuperBully, would become Link Baxter, *Ex*-SuperBully.

CHAPTER EIGHT

Dangerous Duo

The next week was not fun.

Every chance he got, Link did something mean. Like step on my red pen and break it. Or something embarrassing. Like push me into a bunch of fourth-grade girls in the cafeteria. Or something annoying. Like hide my book bag under the seats at the back of the bus.

I was starting to think that Link was a bully because Link was a bully. And I was starting to think there was nothing I could do about it. Except live with it. Every day. For the rest of my life.

Just when I was sure things could not get worse, they did. Thanks to Mrs. Brattle.

Thanksgiving was coming, and we all had to do a social studies project about it. Mrs. Brattle planned all the topics. And Mrs. Brattle wanted everyone to work in pairs. And Mrs. Brattle chose the pairs. And one pair was Jake Drake and Link Baxter. We had to do a report to show how the Native Americans had lived.

Link loved it. He thought it was so funny. A big joke.

He said, "Hey, Flake. This is great. It's you and me. We get to make a teepee together. Tell you what. I'll do the tee part, and you can take care of the pee. Get it? The *pee?*"

Of course, I wanted to tell Link how dumb he was! Because the Native Americans at the first Thanksgiving never saw a teepee. They lived in wetu, round wigwams made of poles and bark. And they made longhouses, too. But you don't say things like that to a SuperBully.

I went up to Mrs. Brattle when everyone else

went to lunch. I said, "Mrs. Brattle, I don't think I should work with Link on the Thanksgiving project."

She said, "Oh? Why is that?"

"Well," I said, "I just think I'd do better with someone else."

Mrs. Brattle said, "I'm sorry, but everyone else is already paired up, Jake. I'm sure you and Link will do just fine."

On the bus home that day, Link said, "That Thanksgiving thing? You're going to do the report, Flake. I don't do dumb stuff like that."

I said, "What do you mean? We're partners."

Link said, "Yeah, right. And you're the partner who has to do the report."

The next day we had library period. I watched Link. He went right to the reference section. He got the *N* encyclopedia. *Good*, I thought. *He's going to look up things about the Native Americans.* Link carried the encyclopedia to a table at the back of the library. My partner was working. Looked good to me.

I went to find some other stuff about Native Americans in Massachusetts.

Near the end of the period I went to show Link the books I found.

He looked up and said, "Great job, Flake."

I said, "What did you find?"

And he said, "Take a look." Behind the encyclopedia Link was reading a book of Garfield cartoons. He said, "I love social studies, don't you?"

So there it was: My partner wasn't just a SuperBully. He was also a moron.

Then it was the day before the project was due.

I had found all the books. I had found all the pictures. I had used my best handwriting to make some labels. I had stuff I could tell about, but we still didn't have a project or anything to show the class.

At the end of the day, Mrs. Brattle said, "Remember, all the Thanksgiving projects are due tomorrow."

So after we got off the bus that afternoon, Link came up to me. He said, "Hey, Flake. Did you finish that dumb report yet?"

And I said, "No. We still have to make something to show about the Native Americans."

And he said, "Well, you better finish it tonight."

It was the way he said it. Like he could just order me around. He thought he could just look at me and make me do whatever he wanted me to. But I was tired of doing all the work. It wasn't fair.

Something inside me snapped. And I said, "No. I'm not going to."

Link took a step closer. He said, "What?"

"I said I'm not going to. I don't care what you say or what you do. I'm not going to make a wigwam or anything else by myself. And if you don't help, then I guess we're just going to get an F on our report."

Link looked down at me with his beady little bully eyes. He clenched his fists. For a second I thought I had made a big mistake. I was about to get pounded into the sidewalk.

Then suddenly, he shrugged. He said, "Fine. Okay. Come over to my house about three-thirty. We'll make a stupid poster or something."

Then he just turned and started walking home.

Standing there in the November sunshine at the corner of Greenwood and Park, I felt like something had changed. It didn't feel like I had killed a dragon or anything.

It was more like back when I was five. Every night I'd thought there was a monster under my bed. And then one night I'd gotten brave enough to look. And it wasn't there. No monster.

But in forty-five minutes I was going to have to go knock on Link's door. Who would open it?

Would it be my social studies partner?

Or a monster?

CHAPTER NINE

Surprises and Questions

Finding Link's house was no problem. He lived in Jimmy Carson's old house, and I had been there plenty of times. I had all the stuff for the project in my book bag.

I went up the front steps and rang the doorbell. I heard a sound. From above. Like *shhhh*.

I looked up just in time to see a fat red water balloon. And above the balloon, Link's head, sticking out of a window on the second floor.

The balloon went *SPLAT* on the steps next to me. Only my shoes got wet. Link laughed and yelled, "Surprise!" Then he said, "Come on in, Flake. Door's open."

My heart was pounding, and I almost turned around and ran for home.

But I didn't. If Link had wanted to put that balloon right on my head, he could have. So that was progress, right? Or was he really trying to soak me, and he just missed?

Anyway, I went inside.

Link's mom was in the front hallway looking through a stack of mail. She must have just gotten home, because her coat was still on. She smiled and said, "Hi. You must be Jake. Link said you were coming over to work on a project. If you get hungry later, you can have a snack."

I said, "Thank you."

Link yelled from the top of the stairs, "Hey! Up here. And bring all your stuff."

Link's room was a surprise. I guess I'd thought it would be like a cave or jail cell or something. It was just a regular room.

There were a lot of comic books around, and there were models on all the shelves. Lots of them. Model cars and trucks and motorcycles. Model ships and airplanes. Even a model train.

I picked up a model of a car.

"Hey! Hands off, Flake."

I put the car down. But I bent over to get a better look.

It was perfect. It was only a plastic model, like the kind at a hobby shop. It had been glued together and then painted bright blue. Perfectly.

I looked at Link. He had flopped onto his bed. He was looking at an *X-Men* comic book.

I said, "This is cool. Where'd you get it?"

"My dad gave me the kit. It's a 1969 Ford Mustang convertible."

I said, "You mean *you* put it together?"

"Yeah," said Link. He didn't take his eyes off the comic book. "I painted it, too."

I could imagine Link having a hobby like collecting wrestling cards. Or catching bugs and spiders. Or maybe throwing glass bottles against a brick wall. But model building? Link?

A girl wearing sweatpants and a green T-shirt came into Link's room. She was tall, with big shoulders and arms, probably in high school. She had about six earrings in each ear, and her hair was brown with a bright pink streak in the front. And she was mad.

She didn't notice me. Real loud, she said, "Hey, Stink."

Link looked up from his comic book. "What?"

"You know what. You took a dollar off my dresser this morning."

"Did not!"

She picked up the Mustang model I had been looking at. She held it out, and started to close her big hand around it.

Link sat up and yelled, "Hey, leave that alone."

She smiled, and her smile looked very familiar to me. Then she said, "Here—catch!" and she tossed the model at Link.

Link caught it before it hit the bed.

The girl said, "I *know* you took that dollar."

Link said, "You probably spent all your money on lipstick or something dumb. And you're so stupid, you probably don't even remember."

She took two steps into the room. "Yeah well,

see if you can remember this, Stink. If I *ever* find you in my room, you are dead." Then she looked at me. "And that goes for your twerpy little friends, too."

Then she left. A few seconds later, a door slammed. Hard.

Link grinned at me and reached over and put the model on the table by his bed. "That's my demented sister."

I got out the book that had some pictures of a Native American village. I was ready to finish this project and go home. Giant girl SuperBullies are not my idea of fun. I said, "Let's get this done, okay?"

Link heaved a bored sigh. "Yeah, okay. I've got some stuff we can use."

He rolled off the bed and walked to a table near the window. There was a big box. It was the kind of box you get new clothes in at Christmas. He pulled off the lid. "We can make something on the inside of this lid."

I said, "Okay."

But I was looking at the things in the box.

There were some brown paper bags, and some sticks and twigs. There were some plastic bags full of sand, and some pieces of dried moss. There were bunches of long green pine needles. And there was some string and some glue.

There was also a page that Link must have ripped out of a *National Geographic* magazine. It showed a painting of a Wampanoag village, complete with wigwams and a longhouse. He had actually done some research.

Link said, "I got most of this junk from my backyard."

"Oh," I said. "So your idea is to make a model village? And to make it look real?"

He looked at me. "Duh. Good thinking, Flake."

I picked up one of the longer sticks. "This could be one of the wigwam poles."

Link shook his head. "Too thick. I got these skinny sticks for that. If they're not skinny, it won't look right."

For the next hour I watched Link work. I tried to help, but I just got in the way.

First Link bent seven or eight skinny sticks to

make a wigwam frame. He tied the sticks together with part of an old shoelace. Then he cut open a big brown bag with scissors. He ripped the brown paper into ragged pieces. He painted little lines all over them. They looked like tree bark. Then he glued the paper onto the wigwam frame.

I showed Link one of the books I brought. He rubbed some black marker onto a paper towel. Then he rubbed that onto the brown paper to make the wigwam look old. Then he glued the whole thing in the box lid.

Then he spread some sand and moss around. He used big stones to look like rocks. He made a little fireplace outside the wigwam with a ring of pebbles. And he used wood and crumpled foil and a red marker to make the fire look real. He made trees and bushes out of the pine needles. And then he made another smaller wigwam. And then he made a longhouse.

It was amazing. It looked like a little village. It looked so good.

Link put down the glue bottle and stepped back a few feet.

I said, "It's really great."

Link shrugged. "It's okay."

I put my things back in my book bag and pulled on my coat. "So you'll bring it to school tomorrow?"

Link snorted. "You think I'm going to let you carry it? And trip and fall all over the place like a doofus? I'll bring it."

I said, "Okay. So I'll see you tomorrow."

Link flopped back onto his bed and picked up another comic book. "Yeah. So long, Flake." Then he said, "Hey, don't forget, Flake. You better do a good job giving this report."

But by then I was halfway down the hall. I tiptoed past his big sister's room and went downstairs. I opened the door, stuck my head out, and looked up. No Link, no water balloons. So I scooted across the steps and headed for home.

I had some stuff I needed to think about.

I had seen a lot at Link's house.

Like his big sister. What would it be like to live in the same house with *that* your whole life?

And his mom. She seemed nice.

And then there was Link.

Sure, he water-bombed me, and he ignored me a lot, and he called me a doofus. But he didn't seem like a SuperBully, at least not all the time. Once in a while, he was just—well, he was just like a kid.

And he was absolutely a great model builder.

I had looked at Link's face while he was thinking about the model. And while he was painting and gluing. When he forgot I was there, he had a different face from his bully face. Not mean. Almost nice.

But when Link remembered I was there, his face would switch back.

So if there's no one to bully, a bully isn't a bully, right?

I couldn't make myself disappear.

But could I make a SuperBully disappear?

That was the question I still could not answer.

CHAPTER TEN

Busted Link

Link wasn't on the bus the next morning. His dad drove him to school with the project.

Right after math in the morning, Mrs. Brattle said, "Now we're going to look at the Thanksgiving projects. First, you should show what you made, and then tell why it's part of the first Thanksgiving story."

Andrea and Laura went first. They had made a poster to show the inside of the *Mayflower*. It looked like their parents had done most of the drawing. And they both talked too soft and giggled a lot.

Then Ben and Carlos showed Plymouth Rock. It was where the Pilgrims had landed. The rock was made of papier-mâché. Except they didn't use enough paint. You could still see the comics and the headlines on the strips of newspaper. But it was an okay report.

And then Mrs. Brattle said, "Jake, Link? You're going to tell us something about the Native Americans."

I said, "Our project is out in the hall under the coatrack."

Link followed me out into the hall. There was a white plastic bag covering the project. The sand and rocks made the box lid heavy. I picked up one end, and Link got the other end. We started toward the door.

Then Link stopped. His face looked pale, and his lips looked blue. In a small voice he said, "I can't do this. Reports. You know, talking to the whole class." He gulped. And then very softly he said, "I can't."

We were face-to-face, about two feet apart. I

was looking up at him. No SuperBully in sight. Just a scared kid. And then I knew why Link had kept telling me that I had to give the report.

Then I felt this rush of power. At last, the great and fearsome Link—completely at my mercy! At last, it was my turn to be the bulliest SuperBully of all!

I could have said, "Oh, wook! It's Wittle Winky—afwaid of a weport!"

I could have said, "So—you make me feel terrible for a whole month, and now you want me to feel sorry for you? Well, too bad, tough guy!"

Or I could have said, "Hurry—let's get in the room so the whole class can see mighty Link Baxter throw up all over the floor—ha, ha, ha!"

But I didn't.

I said, "It'll be okay. Really. All you have to do is stand there and point at stuff when I talk about it. This is a great model. Everyone's going to think it's the best."

Link swallowed hard and took a deep breath. "Okay . . . but you're gonna do the report, right?"

I nodded, and we carried the project into the room and up to the table by the chalkboard.

I looked at a card I had made and said, "We made something to show how the Native Americans lived before the Pilgrims came."

And Link pulled the bag off the model. Some kids in the back stood up so they could see it better. And Mrs. Brattle said, "Everyone should come up closer so you can see. This is really special. Careful, don't bump the table."

The kids were blown away. And so was I. Because after I left his house the day before, Link made some more stuff. He made little bows and arrows. He made some spears and some little baskets, and the baskets had little yellow beads in them, yellow like the color of corn.

So I said, "This is what part of a village looked like. The wigwams and longhouses were made of poles covered with tree bark."

I kept talking, and Link pointed at things. He didn't look like he was going to be sick anymore.

When I was done telling about everything, I said, "And I have to tell the truth. This whole thing? Link made it, and planned it, and he did all the painting, too. I helped a little, but really, Link made it."

And the kids all clapped, and so did Mrs. Brattle. Link's face got red, but he smiled. And it wasn't a bully-smile. It was his real smile.

On the bus home that afternoon, Link sat next to me. But it was different. He didn't poke me or grab my book bag. He just sat there. Like a kid. He joked around with some fourth graders.

When we got off at our stop, I turned toward my house and he turned toward his. But before I turned the corner, he called out, "Hey!"

I cringed. I couldn't help it. It sounded like Link's bully-voice.

He trotted over. No bully-face. He said, "What you did at school today? Thanks." Then he looked all embarrassed. He shrugged and said, "See ya later, Jake."

And I said, "Yeah. See ya."

Then it hit me. Link didn't call me Flake, or Fake. He called me Jake.

So now I'm in fourth grade. And Link still lives around the corner from me. He's even bigger now. I think he might start shaving soon.

It's not like we became best friends or any-thing. He still pretty much thinks I'm a dweeb. And I still pretty much think he's a moron. We never worked on another project together.

And it's not like Link stopped being a bully. But he did stop being a SuperBully. And he never bullied me again. Ever.

I'm still kind of small for my age, still the per-fect size for bullying, and I still look kind of smart, and I haven't turned into a tattletale. But if a kid starts to bully me now, it never lasts. I know too much. Bullies don't fool me anymore. Because back behind those mean eyes and that bully-face, there's another face. A real face.

And if I keep looking for that real face, I see it. And the bully sees me see it.

And *BAM*, just like that, another bully gets busted.

By me. Jake Drake, Bully Buster.

Jake Drake

KNOW-IT-ALL

**To Kathy, Mary, and Frank Despres
in appreciation of their loving, dedicated service
to the children of Westborough**

Contents

CHAPTER ONE   The Catch   1

CHAPTER TWO   Big News   8

CHAPTER THREE   The Rules   16

CHAPTER FOUR   Hunters   23

CHAPTER FIVE   K-I-A/D-I-A   30

CHAPTER SIX   What to Do   36

CHAPTER SEVEN   Secrets and Spies   47

CHAPTER EIGHT   Dropouts   54

CHAPTER NINE   Sticking Together   61

CHAPTER TEN   Teamwork   69

CHAPTER ELEVEN   Winners   77

CHAPTER ONE

The Catch

I'm Jake, Jake Drake. I'm in fourth grade, and I'm ten years old. And I have to tell the truth about something: I've been crazy about computers all my life.

My first computer was an old Mac Classic with a black-and-white screen. I got to play Reader Rabbit and Magic Math. I got to draw pictures on the screen, and I played Battle Tanks. And that was before I could even read.

Then our family got a Mac with a big color monitor. And I got to play Tetris and Shanghai and Solitaire and Spectre. Then I got a joystick for Christmas when I was four, and so did my best friend, Willie. Whenever Willie came to my house we played computer games together. It's not like we played computers all the time, because my mom made a one-hour-a-day rule at my house. But Willie and I filled up that hour almost every day.

Then the computers started getting superfast, and I started messing around with Virtual Drummer, and then SimCity, and SimAnt, and PGA Golf, and about ten other games. And then the Internet arrived at my house, and all of a sudden I could make my computer do some pretty amazing stuff. It was like a magic window.

I'm telling all of this because if I don't, then the rest of this story makes me look like a real jerk. And I'm not a jerk, not most of the time. I just really like computers.

When I started kindergarten, there was a computer in our room. When the teacher saw I was good on it, I got to use it. I even got to teach other kids how to use it. Except for Kevin and

Marsha. They didn't want me to tell them about computers or anything else.

Like I said before, I'm ten now, so I've had some time to figure out some stuff. And one thing I know for sure is this: There's nothing worse than a know-it-all.

Don't get me wrong. I'm pretty smart, and I like being smart. And almost all the kids I know, they're pretty smart, too.

But some kids, they have to prove they're smart. Like, all the time. And not just smart. They have to be the smartest. And that's what Marsha and Kevin are like.

Marsha McCall and Kevin Young were nice enough kids back in kindergarten—as long as I didn't try to tell them anything about the computer. Because when I tried to show Kevin how to make shapes with the drawing program, he said, "I know that." But I don't think he really did. And when I tried to show Marsha how to print out a picture of a kitten, she said, "I can do that myself."

But a lot of the time Kevin and Marsha were pretty nice because kindergarten was mostly playtime.

But when we got to first grade, school changed. All of a sudden there were right answers and wrong answers. And Kevin and Marsha, they went nuts about getting the right answers.

But it was worse than that. They both wanted to get the right answer *first*. It was like they thought school was a TV game show. If you get the right answer first, you win the big prize. Anyway, they both turned into know-it-alls.

Our first-grade teacher was Miss Grimes. Every time she asked a question, Marsha would start shaking all over and waving her hand around and whispering really loud, like this: "Ooh, ooh! I know! I know! I know!"

And while Marsha was going, "Ooh, ooh," Kevin looked like his arm was going to pull his whole body right out of his chair and drag it up to the ceiling, like his arm had its own brain or something.

It was pretty awful. But Miss Grimes, she liked it when Kevin and Marsha tried to be the best at everything. She liked seeing who could get done first with a math problem. She liked

letting everyone with a hundred on a spelling quiz line up first for lunch or recess. First grade felt like a big contest, and Miss Grimes smiled at the winners and frowned at the losers.

When she asked the class a question, most of the time Miss Grimes called on Marsha first. If Marsha was slow or didn't know something, then Kevin got a turn. If Kevin messed up, then she would call on someone else.

And I think I know why Miss Grimes always called on Marsha and Kevin. I think it's because she's kind of a know-it-all herself. I bet she was just like Marsha back when she was in first grade.

Second grade wasn't much better. The only good thing was that my second-grade teacher wasn't like Miss Grimes. Mrs. Brattle didn't want school to be a big contest. So she hardly ever called on the know-it-alls.

All year long, Mrs. Brattle kept saying stuff like, "Kevin and Marsha, please look around at all the other students in this class. They have good ideas, too. Just put your hands down for now."

That didn't stop Kevin and Marsha. The "ooh-oohing" and the arm waving never let up.

But last year, when I was in third grade, that's when things got out of control. And I guess it was partly my fault.

And Mrs. Snavin, my third-grade teacher? She had something to do with it. And so did the principal, Mrs. Karp.

And so did this guy named Mr. Lenny Cordo over at Wonky's Super Computer Store. He had *a lot* to do with it.

Because Mr. Lenny Cordo came to my school one day back when I was in third grade. And Mr. Lenny Cordo told me that he had a present for me. Something really wonderful. Something I had been wishing for.

But there was one small catch. Because there's always at least one small catch.

And this was the catch: Before Mr. Lenny Cordo could give me this wonderful thing that I wanted so much, I would have to do something.

I would have to turn myself into Jake Drake, Know-It-All.

CHAPTER TWO

Big News

When something big is going to happen at school, the kids are always the last to know. First the principal and the teachers and the other grown-ups get everything figured out. Then they tell me and my friends about it. Which doesn't seem very fair, but that's how it happens.

So one Tuesday morning before Christmas vacation, there was an assembly for the kids in third grade, fourth grade, and fifth grade. I sat up front with all the other third graders.

The principal looked huge. Mrs. Karp is

always tall. But standing up on the stage that morning in a green dress, she looked like a giant piece of celery.

There was someone else on the stage. It was this man I had never seen before. He was wearing a yellow sport coat and a purple tie with green polka dots. It was the first time I had ever seen a yellow sport coat. Or a purple tie with green polka dots. I thought maybe he worked for a circus.

He sat on a folding chair, and he had a wide roll of paper lying across his lap. It was noisy in the auditorium. Then Mrs. Karp held up two fingers and leaned toward the microphone.

Mrs. Karp should not be allowed to have a microphone. She doesn't need one. Every kid in the school knows how loud she can yell. When Mrs. Karp yells, it feels like the tiles are going to peel up off the floor and start flying around.

No one wanted to hear Mrs. Karp yell, and especially not into a microphone. So it got quiet in about one second.

Mrs. Karp said, "Good morning, students."

And then she paused.

So all of us said, "Good morning, Mrs. Karp."

Then Mrs. Karp said, "I have some good news this morning. The people at Wonky's Super Computer Store have been talking to our Board of Education. And in just one month, our school is going to have twenty brand-new computers for our media center. *Twenty* new computers—isn't that wonderful?"

Mrs. Karp paused, so all the kids and the teachers in the audience clapped. Some of the fifth graders started cheering and shouting stuff like, "Yaaay!" and, "All riiight!" and, "*Awe*some!"

So Mrs. Karp had to hold up two fingers again. It got quiet right away.

Then she said, "But there's a reason that I've asked just the third-, fourth-, and fifth-grade classes to come here this morning. And that's because during the next-to-last week of January our school is going to have a science fair!"

Mrs. Karp paused again.

But no one clapped this time.

Then she said, "This is the first time we've had a science fair at Despres Elementary School, so this is something brand-new for all of us. And to tell you more about our very first science fair ever, I'd like to introduce Mr. Lenny Cordo. He's the manager of Wonky's Super Computer Store. Mr. Cordo."

The man in the yellow sport coat and the purple tie with green polka dots stood up. He forgot he had that roll of paper on his lap. It dropped onto the floor and rolled off the front of the stage. A lot of kids started laughing. Then Mrs. Karp moved back toward the microphone, and the laughing stopped.

Mrs. Snavin got up from her chair in the front row. She picked up the wide roll of paper and handed it back to the man.

Mr. Lenny Cordo was a lot shorter than Mrs. Karp, so he had to pull the microphone down. Then he said, "Thank you, Mrs. Karp. I am so glad to be here."

That's what Mr. Cordo said, but he didn't look that way. There was sweat all over his forehead, and the roll of paper in his hands was shaking. I guess we looked scary. So he talked fast to get it over with.

"At Wonky's Super Computer Store, we love kids. At Wonky's Super Computer Store, we think it's never too early to get kids excited about science and computers and the future. And that's why Wonky's Super Computer Store is proud to sponsor the First Annual Despres Elementary School Science Fair."

And that's when Mr. Cordo held up the wide piece of paper and let it unroll. It was a banner. It said WONKY'S FIRST ANNUAL ELEMENTARY SCHOOL SCIENCE FAIR.

The biggest word on the banner was "WONKY'S." And the whole banner was upside down.

There was a little laughing, but it stopped because Mr. Cordo kept talking. He wasn't scared anymore. Now he sounded like a guy selling cars on TV.

"In the real world, the world where all of you will live and learn and work in the future, people get rewards for doing good work. And that is why Wonky's Super Computer Store is offering a GRAND PRIZE for the best science fair project in grade three, grade four, and grade five!"

When you say those two words, "GRAND PRIZE," kids pay attention. It got so quiet, I

could almost hear the sweat sliding down Mr. Cordo's forehead. He saw we were listening now, so he took his time.

"That's right. There will be *three* grand prizes for the First Annual Wonky's Science Fair. And do you want to know what each grand prize will be?"

With one giant voice, every kid in the auditorium shouted, "YES!"

So Mr. Cordo leaned closer to the microphone and shouted back. "Then I'm going to tell you! The grand prize for the best science fair project in grade three, grade four, and grade five will be . . . a brand-new Hyper-Cross-Functional Bluntium Twelve computer system!"

I couldn't believe it! For the past three months, the Bluntium Twelve computer had been advertised on every TV channel. And in every magazine and newspaper. I had seen it on billboards and even on the side of a bus.

The Bluntium Twelve was the computer I had been begging my mom and dad to get. It was the fastest computer with the coolest games and the best connections.

It was the computer of my dreams.

All around me kids were clapping and saying stuff like, "Great!" and, "Cool!" and, "Yeah!"

And then I noticed Kevin, and then Marsha. They were sitting in my row of seats.

Kevin and Marsha were not clapping. They were not talking.

Kevin and Marsha were sitting very still. They were thinking.

They were already planning how to win that Bluntium Twelve computer—*my* computer!

And when Mrs. Karp quieted everyone down, I kept looking around, and I could see that other kids were doing the same thing. Kids were starting to think and plan.

Mrs. Karp said some other stuff, but I didn't listen. I was thinking, too.

Because I saw that the only thing standing between me and my very own, superfast, supercool computer was about a hundred other third-grade brains.

But I had a feeling that the only other brains I really had to worry about belonged to those two know-it-alls—Kevin Young and Marsha McCall.

CHAPTER THREE

The Rules

After the assembly about the science fair, our classroom was noisy.

Mrs. Snavin came in and said, "Everyone please sit in your chairs. I have something to give you."

Eric Kenner said, "Is it a computer?"

Everybody laughed, even Mrs. Snavin.

She said, "No, it's not a computer, Eric. But it *is* some news about the science fair."

That got things quiet fast.

"Now," said Mrs. Snavin, "the first thing you all need to know is that no one has to be part of the science fair. This is something you can choose to do, or choose not to do. It will be good experience, but it will not make any difference in your grades either way."

While she was talking, Mrs. Snavin took a pile of papers from her desk and started passing them out.

She said, "This is about the science fair. You should take this booklet home and read it with your mom or dad. There is a form that you and a parent will have to sign. Bring it back to me before Christmas vacation if you are going to enter the science fair. You should pay special attention to page three. That's the page that tells the kinds of projects that are allowed, and the kinds of projects you should not make."

It was dead quiet in the room except for the rustling of paper.

I got my booklet and started to flip through it. It had ten pages, and it all looked pretty boring. I started to fold it up so I could put it in my backpack to take home.

But then I looked at Kevin. He was hunched over his desk, reading fast. He had a pencil and

he was making little check marks and notes on the pages.

Then I turned my head toward the other side of the room and looked at Marsha. Same thing, except she was using a pink Hi-Liter.

Usually, I would have looked at Marsha and Kevin and said to myself, *know-it-alls.*

But not that day. I grabbed my red pen, I unfolded my science fair papers, and I started reading. No way was I going to let either of those kids get my Bluntium Twelve computer.

Then Mrs. Snavin said, "Are there any questions about the science fair?"

Right away Kevin's hand went up.

Mrs. Snavin said, "Yes, Kevin?"

"Can kids work together on the science fair?"

Mrs. Snavin started flipping pages in the information packet. She said, "On page nine it says, 'Students may work on a science fair project alone or with one partner.'"

Then I put my hand up. Mrs. Snavin nodded at me, so I said, "But what if two kids make a project, and it wins first place. Would both kids get a prize?"

Mrs. Snavin flipped some more pages. Then she said, "On page six it says, 'Only one grand prize will be awarded for the winning project in grade three, grade four, and grade five.' So the answer is no, Jake. If a team won first place, I guess they would have to figure out how to share the prize or split it up someway."

So that was that. I had to work by myself. No way was I going to split my new computer with anybody else.

Mrs. Snavin said, "Any other questions?"

Two more kids put up their hands—Pete Morris and Marsha. Marsha got called on first.

Whenever Marsha talked, everything sounded like a question.

She said, "On page seven? Well, it says I have to get my project idea approved? Before I start working on it? Well, what if I want to start working on it today? Like, after school today? And tonight?" Mrs. Snavin smiled. "I think you'd better wait until you talk with your mom or dad before you begin, Marsha. And don't worry. There will be plenty of time."

You see that? How Mrs. Snavin said "there will

be plenty of time"? And how she said "don't worry"? That's because Mrs. Snavin didn't get it. She didn't understand how know-it-alls have to get the right answer. Or about how they always have to be first. Or how they always worry.

Pete Morris still had his hand up. So Mrs. Snavin called on him.

Pete's a science kid. He knows every kind of bug there is. Even their fancy names, and which bug is related to which other bug, and what they eat and how long they live. Pete's really smart.

Pete said, "I think insects would be a good science fair topic. Because I have a lot of different bugs. Bugs are my hobby. And rocks, too. And also worms and plants. And sometimes different kinds of monkeys. So, is it okay to have your science fair project and your hobby be the same thing?"

Mrs. Snavin said, "That's a good question, Pete, and the answer is yes. But I still think you all need to talk to your moms or dads, and they can help you decide what's best for you to do. Now, that's all the time we have for this today."

Then it was quiet reading time, so we all put

the science fair stuff away and got out our library books.

Except I didn't. And neither did Marsha. She put the science fair papers down in her lap where she could keep reading them.

And I didn't even bother to look over at Kevin. I knew he was still thinking about the science fair, too.

And me? I kept the papers out on my desk. That way I could look down at them under my library book. I needed to get to work. Maybe I could go to the library after lunch. Then I could get a head start.

Because I wanted to be the first. And the best. I wanted to win.

And I didn't just want to win. I *had* to win.

I had to be know-it-all number one.

CHAPTER FOUR

Hunters

By lunchtime, I had read everything about the science fair. Twice. I was ready to work.

So I waited until just before lunch. I waited until Mrs. Snavin was alone at her desk. Then I went up and asked for a library pass for after lunch. And I kind of whispered. And when she gave me the pass, I hid it in my hand.

But Marsha saw it anyway. Because Marsha was watching me like a cat watches a hamster. And right away, she jumped up and rushed over to the teacher's desk. She said, "Mrs. Snavin?

A library pass? Could I have one, too?"

Except Marsha didn't whisper. So three seconds later, Kevin also had a library pass.

Because that's the way it is, and you have to get used to it. Know-it-alls are usually copycats, too.

After lunch, the library was like a know-it-all convention. All the smart kids were there. Plus all the kids who thought they were smart. Plus all the kids who wanted everyone else to think they were smart. Plus me.

We were all there. Everyone wanted a head start. Everyone wanted to win.

The only good thing was that not all the kids there were in third grade. Besides me and Marsha and Kevin, there were only three other third graders.

And Pete Morris wasn't one of them. I looked out the window and I saw Pete. He was out by the bushes near the fence. He was bending over. He was looking at one of the branches.

But my best friend, Willie, was in the library. His real name is Phil, but his last name is Willis, so everyone calls him Willie, even his teachers. Willie's third-grade teacher was Mrs. Frule.

When Willie saw me, he smiled and came over to my table. "Hey," he said, "isn't it great? I mean about the computer? I would love to have that thing in my room. Got any good ideas yet? I think I might try to build a bridge or something like that, you know? Something big. How about you? What do you want to do?"

But all I said was, "Listen, Willie, I've got to get to work now, okay?"

"Sure," said Willie, "but I thought maybe we could be partners. We could make something totally . . . you know, like, totally . . . total."

Willie was great at starting sentences. Finishing them was the hard part.

I shook my head. "Won't work, Willie. What if what we make wins first prize? Then what?"

Willie looked at me like I was nuts. "Then we'll have this cool computer, that's what. We can keep it at your house some of the time, and at my house some of the time. It'll be great!"

I shook my head again. "I don't think so, Willie. I think we better just do our own stuff."

Willie shrugged. "Okay. But if I win, I'll still let you use my computer sometimes, okay?"

I smiled and said, "Sure. That'll be great."

But inside, to myself, I said, *You? Win the science fair? Forget about it, Willie. That grand prize is* mine.

Which was not very nice. But when you have to get the right answer, and you have to get it first, and you have to win, then you don't have as much time to be nice anymore.

When Willie walked away, I looked at the papers about the science fair again. There was a part that said you couldn't make a project that used fire or acid. For electricity, you could only use batteries. And you couldn't use chemicals that might explode or make smoke.

Those rules knocked a lot of fun stuff off the list.

In the booklet it said there would be five judges. So I tried to think like a science fair judge. But I got tired of that. It was hard enough to think like a third grader.

I grabbed my papers and went over to a computer that was hooked up to the Internet. I sat down, clicked on "search," and then typed in "science fair projects."

In two seconds, I got a message. It said 206,996 Web pages matched with my search! And the first ten links were on the screen.

So I clicked on a link that said "Science Fair Helper." Sounded like the right stuff. And it was. It had some good things, so I clicked on a second link. And that second link had some good ideas, too. And so did the third link, and the fourth, and the fifth.

Then it hit me—there was probably a good idea on every page, all 206,996 of them! But I didn't need 200,000 ideas. I just needed one. I needed *my* idea.

I felt something. Behind me. I turned around real quick, and guess what? It was Kevin Young. He had come up right behind me and he was staring at the screen. My screen.

"Hey!" I said. "What are you doing, Kevin?"

Kevin shrugged. "Nothing."

I said, "Then go do nothing somewhere else."

Kevin had red hair, and his face was freckled, and his eyes were this real pale blue. And he didn't blink much.

Kevin stuck out his chin and said, "I can be anywhere I want to in the library. And you know, it's against the rules to copy a project from the Internet."

And from around the end of some shelves, suddenly Marsha was standing there next to Kevin. She nodded her head so her ponytail bobbed up and down. "That's right, what Kevin said? About copying? How it's, like, cheating?"

It was hard not to get mad. Real mad.

But all I said was, "What? Do you think I'm stupid? I know not to cheat. Just mind your own business, both of you. You know what things look like right now? It looks like you two are copying ideas from *me*, that's what it looks like."

They left, and I was still pretty mad.

But when I thought about it later, I felt better . . . about Kevin and Marsha watching out for me, I mean. I was something they weren't so sure about. It made me feel good because if they were worried about me, that meant I was worth worrying about.

Jake Drake was something those know-it-alls didn't know about, and they both knew it.

CHAPTER FIVE
K-I-A/D-I-A

That night after dinner I told my mom and dad about the science fair. We were having ice cream for dessert. Mom and I had chocolate, and Dad and Abby had vanilla and strawberry. Abby's my little sister. She's two years younger than I am. So back then, when I was in third grade, Abby was a first grader.

I handed the science fair booklet to my dad. Right away he flipped through it. He looked at each page for about two seconds.

He said, "Okay . . . yeah . . . that makes

sense . . . this is good . . . fine. Great, Jake. This'll be a lot of fun."

Then he ripped the permission slip off the back page. He signed his name and handed his pen to me. "Just sign on the line, Jake . . . there you go. Now we're all set. So what do you think? You want to make a rocket? Or maybe a volcano? Those are a lot of fun. Or maybe a model of a planet? I always loved making Saturn, you know? The one with all the rings? That's a great project."

Meanwhile, my mom started reading the booklet. Carefully.

Abby wasn't doing anything except stirring her ice cream around and around in her bowl.

Mom said, "My goodness! Jim, did you see that there's a prize for first place?"

"Well, of course . . . well, sure," Dad said. "There's always a prize for first place. When I won my seventh-grade science fair, I got a nice trophy. But I think my sister threw it out when I went to college."

My mom winked at me. Then she said to Dad, "Okay. You know there's a prize. But do you know what the prize is?"

My dad said, "Well . . . no, I mean, not exactly. But I know there's a prize, so we'll try to win it—right, Jakey? Like with a rocket, something really exciting. The judges love exciting projects."

Mom had flipped to another page. She looked sideways at me and said, "Jake, why don't you tell your dad why you will not be making a rocket for the science fair."

I said, "That's because on page three it says I can't make anything that burns, or smokes, or explodes."

Dad said, "Well . . . there *are* other kinds of rockets . . . like the kind that use water power. You know, a water rocket? So, we could still make a rocket."

Mom laughed and said, "That sounds like something a K-I-A/D-I-A might say."

I said, "What's that mean . . . K-I-A/D-I-A?"

Abby looked up from her ice-cream soup. She said, "I know. It means Know-It-All/Do-It-All. Mommy told me."

And I remembered that I had heard Mom say that before.

One time Dad wouldn't read about how to put

a new bicycle together. Mom said he was being a K-I-A/D-I-A.

And when we got a new garage door opener, it broke because Dad hooked the motor on backwards. He didn't read the instructions. When that happened, Mom said, "Dear, sometimes I wish you weren't such a K-I-A/D-I-A."

Or when my dad wouldn't stop and ask for directions when we were lost in the car? I heard Mom say, "Don't be a K-I-A/D-I-A."

Mom handed the booklet back to Dad, and he started reading.

I said, "You know the prize? It's amazing, Dad. If I win first prize, I get a Bluntium Twelve computer! From Wonky's Super Computer Store."

Dad said, "A whole system? A Bluntium Twelve?"

"Yeah," I said, "and a year of free Internet service, too!"

Dad whistled.

And then Abby tried to whistle, too. But instead, some melted ice cream drooled down her chin.

Dad looked at the booklet again. He said,

"Well, I guess we had better get right to work on this, eh, Jake?"

See that? How my dad said "we"? He said, ". . . *We* had better get right to work. . . ."

That "we" got me worried. This was supposed to be *my* science fair. Right in the science fair booklet it said that kids had to do their own work.

And then I thought, *What if Dad thinks he's going to get a new computer when my project wins first prize?*

Kids like Kevin and Marsha? I knew they were going to be a problem. I was ready for that.

But what if your dad is a K-I-A—and a D-I-A, too?

How do you tell your own dad to keep hands off? And that you don't want to share your new computer with anyone—not even him?

On this science fair project, there was only room for one K-I-A.

And that was me.

CHAPTER SIX

What to Do

After dessert, I took the science fair booklet to my room. It had some ideas about choosing what to do.

The rules said I had to use *the scientific method*. Which works like this:

First you look around the world and see something interesting. That's called *observation*.

After you look around, you ask a question about something. That part's called the *question*. Which makes sense.

Then you make a guess about the answer.

When you do a science fair project, your guess is called a *hypothesis*. But it's still a guess.

Then you plan out some trials to test and see if your guess is right or wrong. That part is called the *method*.

Then you do your testing, and you write down what you find out. That's called the *result*.

And then you have to tell if your guess was right or wrong. That's called the *conclusion*.

But I was stuck way back at the beginning. I was having trouble with the question part. So I kept reading and the science fair booklet said:

Try filling in these blanks to make a question you want to explore:

What is the effect of _____ on

_____?"

And then it gave two examples:

What is the effect of __dishwasher soap__ on __grass__ __seedlings__?

What is the effect of __total darkness__ on __how__ __much gerbils sleep__?

So I tried filling in some words of my own.

**What is the effect of _ sawdust _ on _ the taste of a _
 vanilla milkshake _?**
**What is the effect of _ a dead cockroach _ on _ Abby's _
 pillow at bedtime _?**
**What is the effect of _ a red hot pepper _ on _ Willie's _
 peanut butter sandwich _?**

I liked my questions.

And after you ask a question, you have to make a guess. So I gave that a try too:

**—Sawdust would make a vanilla milkshake taste
like . . . plywood?**
**—A dead cockroach on Abby's pillow at bedtime
would . . . cause loud screams and a lot of yelling,
and make me be grounded with no TV or computer
games for three weeks.**
**—And a red hot pepper on Willie's peanut butter
sandwich would . . . make Willie jump up from his
chair, drink six cartons of chocolate milk, and then
throw up all over the cafeteria.**

Pretty good guesses.

But I had to stop messing around.

So I lay down on my bed and looked at the ceiling. My ceiling has all these swirls and ridges. It's like looking at clouds. Sometimes I can see all kinds of stuff up there. But that night I didn't see anything. Just a big white blank.

Deciding what to do for a science fair is hard. It's hard because what you really have to do is choose what *not* to do.

Because you could do anything. You could do millions of different things.

Except you can only do one thing.

So after you choose all the stuff *not* to do, then you look at what's left over. And that's what you do.

I got up and went over to my dresser and opened the top drawer. It's my junk drawer. That's what my mom calls it because it all looks like junk to her.

And then I got an idea. Maybe I could find an idea by looking at my junk. All of it.

So I grabbed my notebook from my backpack.

I opened it to an empty page. I found a pencil. Then I looked into my junk drawer and I started making a list.

7 paper clips

3 big paper clips

9 old batteries

1 twisty pencil sharpener

1 orange golf ball

1 toenail clippers

2 wooden yo–yos

1 plastic yo–yo with no string

13 rubber bands

4 Hot Wheels

18 baseball cards

6 of Willie's basketball cards

3 pens

29 colored pencils

7 keys that I don't know what they fit

17 crayons

9 marbles

1 plastic magnifying glass

2 mini–superballs

half a pair of dice

1 piece of chain from a broken lamp

1 little lock, no key

1 red magnet shaped like a horseshoe

1 broken glow–in–the–dark watch

1 mini Frisbee

37 pennies

1 empty Altoids tin with 1 Canadian quarter

1 roll of thin wire

1 red stamp pad

1 fingernail file

1 plastic ruler

1 Mickey Mouse PEZ holder

1 pink eraser

1 white eraser

1 fishing bobber

1 piece of a radio antenna

1 cracked candy cane

6 pen caps

1 film container with 43 blue beads

2 computer disks

3 mini–screwdrivers

1 mini–stapler

1 broken snail shell

1 plastic ring from a gum ball machine

3 red plastic pushpins

1 flashlight, doesn't work

4 short pencils, no erasers

1 roll of Scotch tape

3 butterscotch Life Savers
1 chain dog collar
3 rusty bolts
1 plastic bottle of white glue
1 Hacky Sack with a hole, blue beads leaking out
3 gray stones
2 pieces of green glass from the beach
1 pair of scissors with orange handles
1 mini Etch-A-Sketch on a key ring
1 eye off my old toy cat Fluffy
4 Star Wars action figures
1 broken camera
3 suction cups off of Garfield's paws
1 small, brown glass bottle
1 white shoelace

3 little seashells from Florida
1 round mirror from Mom's makeup
1 plastic bubble wand
2 root beer bottle caps
1 big nail
4 ribbons I won at YMCA camp
3 small nails, all rusty
1 old toothbrush
1 calculator
1 little roll of white string
1 plastic harmonica
1 short measuring tape
1 jingle bell off of my Christmas stocking
1 sand timer from a game
1 cork
1 wire key ring
1 pair of pliers

And then I stopped. There was still more stuff, but I was tired of writing. Plus I didn't want to use another piece of paper. Plus I felt like I was just wasting time.

I was almost ready to go and ask my dad for help. That would be dangerous, because of that K-I-A/D-I-A thing. That might be bad, but it would be better than never finding an idea at all.

But as I stared at all that stuff, I remembered something.

I remembered how I'd read in this kids' magazine about magnets. About how you can wrap wire around something made of iron. Then if you run electricity through the wire, it makes a magnet.

I pushed a bunch of things out of the way until I found the big nail. It was about four inches long. Then I found the roll of thin wire. Starting at the head of the nail, I began winding wire around and around, onto the nail. There wasn't that much wire. Still, I put about thirty turns on the nail before it ran out.

Then I grabbed the toenail clippers. I peeled some of the plastic cover off one end of the wire. Then I found the other end of the wire. I peeled some plastic off that end, too.

Now I needed power. I reached into the drawer and pulled out a big fat flashlight battery. I pressed one end of the wire on the top, and the other end on the bottom of the battery. Then I put the end of the nail near a small paper clip. And . . . nothing. Zero. Zilch.

I threw the nail and the wire and the battery into the drawer and started to shut it.

Then I thought, *Hey, you idiot! It's probably a dead battery—try again!*

I poked around in the drawer until I found one of those small boxy batteries, like the kind from a walkie-talkie. I hooked one end of the wire to each little button on the battery. I moved the nail next to a paper clip, and *zzip!* It jumped right onto the nail! And so did three other paper clips, and so did a bottle cap, and so did the fingernail file!

So then I looked at this wire and battery and nail. And I looked at the stuff dangling from the nail. And I said to myself, *Okay, but does this help with my science fair? This is just stupid stuff from my junk drawer.*

I looked at the science fair booklet again, at the question part, where it said:

What is the effect of_____**on**

_____**?**

So I asked. I asked myself,

"What is the effect of _more batteries_ on _the_ _power of the magnet_ ?"

And then I asked myself,

"What is the effect of _more wire_ on _the power of_ _the magnet_ ?"

And then I thought,

"What makes more difference, more wire or more batteries?"

And the great part was, I really wanted to know the answer!

You know how sometimes you can just see something in your head? Just see it like it was all right there? That's how it was.

I could see this big poster telling all about my idea. And another one telling how I tested my idea, and what results I got.

I could see these big supermagnets I made. They were all hooked up to batteries, humming like the lights at school. And my magnets were lifting up these heavy chunks of metal.

I could see myself at the science fair. I could see the judges listening to me explain everything. They were smiling.

I could see Kevin and Marsha. They were *not* smiling.

And I could see me sitting in my room. I was playing ZEE-SQUADRON STRIKE FORCE on my new Bluntium Twelve computer.

It was so simple.

All I had to do was make those things happen in real life. That's all.

CHAPTER SEVEN

Secrets and Spies

I learned a lot during that week before Christmas vacation.

I learned about the science fair and the grand prize. I learned that Mr. Lenny Cordo did not work for a circus. I learned that I wanted to win that Bluntium Twelve computer. I learned that sometimes my dad can be a K-I-A/D-I-A. I learned about the scientific method.

And I learned that just because you're in third grade, it doesn't mean you can't read some long words.

Like "electromagnets." That's the fancy name for the kind of magnets you make with wire and iron and electricity. That's something else I learned. Because the rest of that week before Christmas, I read all I could about magnets.

And another thing I learned is that a know-it-all can't really be a know-it-all. Nobody can know *everything*. There's too much. If you did know everything, your head would explode or something.

But I guess nobody ever told that to Kevin and Marsha. They really wanted to know everything, all the time.

But there was something they didn't know. And they knew they didn't know it.

They didn't know what my science fair project was.

At first, Kevin tried to pretend he didn't care. The day before vacation, we had to turn in our permission slips. Mrs. Snavin told us to bring them to her desk. I stood up, and Kevin got in line behind me. I could tell he did it on purpose.

Kevin tapped me on the shoulder. When I turned around, he gave me this fake smile and said,

"So, Jake, what are you doing your project on?"

I said, "I don't think I want to tell anybody."

He said, "Why not? It doesn't matter if people know. I'm doing mine on ants."

Kevin stared at me with his pale blue eyes. He didn't blink. He was waiting for me to tell. Especially since he had just told me what his project was.

But I just smiled and nodded. I said, "Ants. Yeah, ants are cool." And then I turned away because I had to hand my slip to Mrs. Snavin.

Kevin followed me back to my table. "So what's your project, Jake?"

I said, "I'm still kind of thinking about it."

Kevin said, "So what is it? What are you thinking about?"

I said, "I'll show you at the science fair."

Kevin pressed his lips together and made a mad face. Then he walked back to his own table.

You see, I'm a good secret keeper.

Two years ago, Abby broke a little china statue my mom had on a shelf. Mom loved it because she said it looked like Abby. That's why Abby loved it, too.

One day Abby pushed a chair over to the shelf and she took it down. When she started playing with it, the head broke off.

Abby brought it to me. She was crying. She was afraid she would get in big trouble. I used some white glue to put the head back on. I was very careful. You couldn't even tell it was broken. I put it back on the shelf. And I promised I would keep it a secret. And I did.

Of course, about a week later, Abby told Mom about the statue herself. And Mom wasn't even mad. Even so, I kept the secret.

And then there was the time a friend of mine was at the YMCA camp with me. In the middle of the night he woke me up. He whispered, "Jake . . . I . . . I wet my bed. What should I do?"

That's the kind of thing a kid can get a bad nickname for. So I helped him get the sheet off his bunk. It was a plastic mattress, so that was good. I got my extra sheet out of my trunk, and we put it on the mattress. Then we stuck the wet sheet under his bed and went back to sleep.

No one ever found out, and I never told.

And don't even try to guess which friend it

was, because I'm not telling. Ever. It's a secret.

So I decided my science fair project was going to be a secret, too. Why tell anybody? Especially Kevin Young.

And Marsha? She never asked. She just snooped. And she was lousy at it. It was like I had radar. I could always tell when Marsha was trying to spy on me.

So I let her see me work, and I let Kevin see me, too. It was during our library period on the last day before vacation. I let Marsha see me check out a book on snakes.

Then I let Kevin see me looking at stuff about sharks in the encyclopedia.

Then I used *Encarta* to look up an article about weasels, and I left it on the computer screen a long time. I even took some notes. And Marsha saw me.

Then, ten minutes later, when Kevin was waiting at the printer, I printed out this article about rodents with a big picture of a rat. When I went to get it, Kevin handed it to me with a smile.

And I smiled back.

Near the end of the library time, I saw Kevin

and Marsha whispering together. They looked like they were arguing. Kevin probably thought my project was about rats and sharks, and Marsha probably thought I was studying snakes and weasels.

They didn't get my joke. What I did was study *them*. And I had discovered that Kevin reminded me of a cross between a shark and a rat, and Marsha was like a snake and a weasel.

What they didn't know was that in the bottom of my backpack, down in a safe dark place, I had three great books: *All About Magnets*; *Magnets You Can Make*; and *Winning Science Fair Projects*. And those three books were enough to help me win my new computer.

Because the best thing I learned that week before vacation was this: To be a good know-it-all, you don't have to know what anybody else is doing. And you don't need to know everything. You just have to know enough.

Plus it helps if you have a big drawer full of junk.

CHAPTER EIGHT

Dropouts

Then it was Christmas vacation. That's always been my favorite time of year. Where we live, there's almost always snow at Christmas. And there's nothing better than snow plus no school.

But this vacation was different.

On Christmas morning I was waiting at the top of the stairs with Abby. Was I thinking about all the presents under the tree in the living room? No. I was thinking about magnets.

And after the big Christmas dinner, and after Gram and Grampa went home, did I play with my new LEGO motor kit for the rest of the afternoon? No. I dug around in Dad's workshop. I was looking for wire and pieces of iron.

And it was like that all week. Every day I did some work on my project. I read my books. I made some drawings. I used the scientific method and I wrote things down.

One day I had Mom take me to the hardware store. We bought four big batteries. Each one was as heavy as a jar of peanut butter—a full one. We bought two of the biggest nails I had ever seen. They were about a foot long, and thicker than my pointer finger. And then we went to RadioShack and bought two big spools of thin wire.

That was what my vacation was like. When I wasn't working on my project, I was thinking about it.

I mean, I didn't work on it the whole week, not every second. One day I went sledding with Willie. We had a great time, and we didn't talk about our projects, not even once.

And I did build this amazing LEGO machine. Which Abby wrecked.

So even a big science fair project can't ruin Christmas. But it came pretty close.

The week after vacation, Kevin went from being a know-it-all to a show-it-all. You know how I worked to keep my project a secret? Kevin worked even harder to show and tell everyone about his. All the time.

If kids walked past Kevin's table, he would start telling all about his ants. And if they tried to walk away, he'd say, "And look what else I found out!"

Kevin worked on a big poster at the table by the windows. He just left it lying there for everyone to see. The poster was great, it really was— and it wasn't even half done.

In the gym on Tuesday, Kevin lay down on the floor by the wall. He started looking at some ants with a magnifying glass. They were in a long line, marching toward the door to the cafeteria. When kids came around, he told about how he had found out the way ants smell things. And how their eyes and jaws work.

And Kevin brought these amazing pictures. He took them with a digital camera. He printed them out on the color printer during library period. He showed them to everybody.

On Thursday I was waiting in line with Willie to buy ice-cream sandwiches. I said, "So did you start your project over vacation?"

He said, "Yeah, I got some done. But I'm not going to be in the science fair. And four other kids in my class, they're quitting, too."

I didn't understand. I said, "What do you mean?" Willie peeled back the paper and bit off a corner of his ice-cream sandwich. He said, "I quit the science fair. It's too much trouble. Besides, everybody knows Kevin's going to win."

I was still confused, and Willie could tell.

He said, "You've seen Kevin's stuff about ants, right? It's really good. And so is Karl Burton's stuff. In my class? His project is about simple machines. But I think Kevin's is better."

And then I got it. I got what Kevin had been doing all week.

I said, "Don't you see, Willie? Don't you see? That's what Kevin wants. He's been showing off his science project so kids like us will drop out. He set a trap, and you walked into it!"

Willie shrugged. "Yeah, I guess so. But what's the point? It wasn't any fun to work on."

Willie kept squeezing the ice cream out of the middle of his ice-cream sandwich so he could lick it off.

I said, "But what about the Bluntium Twelve? And a whole year of free Internet? Don't you want to win that?"

Willie shrugged again. "I mean, sure. That would be great. But I don't really *need* a new computer. And who wants to just try to beat Kevin all the time?"

That made me think. And I got madder and madder at Kevin. He didn't really break any rules, but what he was doing didn't seem fair.

And I got mad at Marsha because she was as bad as Kevin. All week long she had been telling everyone about her project, too. She was going to prove that she could fool grass seeds into growing upside down.

And then I got mad at Mr. Lenny Cordo. I thought it was all his fault that everyone was so upset about the science fair. Everyone was going nuts about his new computers.

And then I got mad at Mrs. Karp and Mrs.

Snavin and all the other grown-ups. They were the ones who let Wonky's Super Computer Store talk them into this whole idea.

And when I ran out of other people to get mad at, I got mad at myself.

I had turned myself into a know-it-all. I had gotten as mean as Kevin and as sneaky as Marsha. I had practically ruined Christmas so I could win the big prize.

But, worst of all, back when Willie wanted to be my partner, what did I do? I sent him off on his own. I threw him into the shark tank with Kevin and into the snake pit with Marsha. Willie and I could have had fun working on a project. Together.

All Thursday afternoon my thoughts went around and around. I got sick of the whole mess. And I decided there was only one thing to do.

I was going to forget about Kevin and Marsha.

I was going to forget about Mrs. Karp and Mrs. Snavin.

I was going to forget about Mr. Lenny Cordo. And his Bluntium Twelve computer.

I was going to quit the stupid science fair, too, just like my best friend, Willie.

CHAPTER NINE

Sticking Together

After I talked with Willie on Thursday afternoon, I felt like quitting the science fair. I really did.

I didn't talk to anyone on the bus after school. When I got home, I went right to my room.

Books and papers were spread all over the top of my desk. I had big batteries and spools of wire and giant nails spread around on the floor. I had markers and poster boards sticking out from under my bed.

The more I looked at all that stuff, and the more I thought about Willie, the madder I got.

And right then, I knew I couldn't quit. I just couldn't. I couldn't let Kevin and Marsha push everyone out of the way.

Then I got an idea. I looked around on my desk until I found the science fair booklet. Then I read the rules again. And for the first time in three or four hours, I smiled.

On Friday morning, I had my dad drive me to school. That way, I got there about ten minutes before the buses. I didn't talk much in the car.

When we were almost there, Dad said, "So, how's the science fair coming? It's next week, right?"

I shook my head. "Nope. It's the week after. And I guess it's okay."

"Anything I can help with? I've never made electromagnets, but I think I understand how they work."

I smiled and said, "Thanks, but I'm supposed to do the work myself. It says that in the rules."

We pulled up at the front door of the school. Dad said, "I'm sure you're doing a terrific job.

But maybe I could at least look things over."

I said, "Sure. That'd be good."

Dad leaned over and gave me a kiss on the cheek. "Have a great day, Jake."

I went into the office and asked Mrs. Drinkwater for permission to go to my room before the first bell. Mrs. Drinkwater is the school secretary. She's a good person to know. Even though Mrs. Karp is the principal, I think Mrs. Drinkwater runs my school most of the time. Because if you want to find out anything, you talk to Mrs. Drinkwater. Unless you're in trouble. Then you talk to Mrs. Karp.

When I got to my room, Mrs. Snavin was sitting at her desk using a calculator.

I guess my shoes were too quiet, because when I said, "Mrs. Snavin?" she jumped about a foot and let out this little squeal. "Oooh!—It's you, Jake. That gave me a fright."

I said, "Sorry, Mrs. Snavin. But I have to talk with you. You know Willie, my friend in Mrs. Frule's class? I want to be partners with him for the science fair."

Mrs. Snavin frowned. "The fair is the week

after next. I think it's a little late to be choosing up partners."

I reached into my backpack and pulled out the science fair booklet. I said, "It doesn't say anywhere in here that you have to pick partners by a special time. It just says that you have to sign up on time, and it says you can work by yourself or with one partner. And Willie and I both signed up before Christmas."

Mrs. Snavin was still frowning. "Why has it taken this long to decide you want to work together?"

I said, "That's my fault. Willie wanted to be partners right at the start, but I said no. But now I want to. So will it be okay?"

Mrs. Snavin took a deep breath and let it out slowly. She was looking through my booklet. "Well . . . it doesn't seem to be against the rules. So, it'll be all right. I'll get the master list from the office and change it later today."

I said, "Thanks, Mrs. Snavin." Then I went back to the side doors to wait for the buses.

Willie was on bus four, but it was a while before he got off.

"Hey, Willie! Over here!"

He saw me and waved. He moved through the crowd of kids to where I was waiting. "Hi, Jake!"

We walked into the gym, and I said, "Guess what?"

"What?" he said.

"I've got a new partner for the science fair."

Willie looked at me and squinted. "What do you mean? Who?"

I grinned. "You! You're back in the science fair. You're my partner!"

Willie said, "No way!"

And I said, "Way! I talked with Mrs. Snavin already, and it's not against the rules or anything."

Willie smiled this smile that almost covered his whole face.

Then the smile stopped, and he squinted again. "But you said you wanted to work by yourself."

I said, "Yeah, but now I don't. I wasn't having much fun, either."

The first bell rang, and everyone began to move for the doors.

I said, "Tell you what. Get a pass to go to the library for lunch recess, and we can talk about it, okay?"

Willie said, "Yeah . . . okay. See you in the library." And then he smiled his big smile again. It's a great smile.

When you have a partner to work with, and it's a good partner, everything is more fun. It just is.

After Willie and I talked at the library we decided to work on the magnets. He had been making a project about how different balls bounce. It's because Willie loves basketball and almost every sport. He's not very good at sports, but he still loves them. So he wanted to observe Ping-Pong balls, golf balls, tennis balls, and basketballs bouncing. Then he wanted to guess why they bounced in different ways, and then try to prove it.

It was kind of an interesting idea, but Willie hadn't done much with it.

When I told him about the electromagnets, he got all excited. "You mean a regular nail turns into a magnet?"

I said, "Yeah, only I've got two giant nails this

long! And you know at a junkyard? They have electromagnets on the end of a crane that can pick up whole cars, and when they shut off the power, BAM, the whole car falls to the ground!"

Then I told him about everything we had to do. And Willie got more and more excited. He said he would ask his mom if he could come over on Saturday. Then we could work all day on it.

"That'll be great. And there's one more thing," I said. "I've been keeping the project a secret. Especially from Kevin and Marsha."

Willie nodded slowly and began to grin. "Yeah. I like it. That means we know something that they don't know, right?"

See what I mean? How Willie got the idea right away?

Me and Willie are like that. We're good partners. We laugh at the same kinds of stuff, and when he needs help or I need help, we stick together.

Like magnets.

CHAPTER TEN

Teamwork

You know how people say "two heads are better than one"? Well, it's true, especially if the other head is Willie's head.

When he came over to my house on Saturday morning, we got right to work. First, I showed Willie what I had written down. And I told him how it was my idea to see what made a magnet more powerful: more wire or more batteries. I had the idea, but I hadn't a guess about it yet. In the scientific method, that's called the hypothesis.

Willie looked at the stuff, and he looked at my notes. Then he said, "More electricity makes an electromagnet stronger than more wire."

I said, "How do you know that?"

Willie shook his head. "I don't. That's our hypothesis. 'More electricity makes an electromagnet stronger than more wire.' We have to prove whether that's true or false."

See what I mean about two heads? In a minute, Willie had a big part of the problem all worked out. I wrote the hypothesis in our notebook. Then came the fun part. I know that might sound weird, but making those electromagnets was really fun.

We talked and we argued about stuff, and we tried six different ways of winding wire on the nails. And Willie figured out a great way to keep track of how much wire we were using.

We decided to put 150 feet of red wire onto one of the nails. We would put 300 feet of blue wire onto the other nail. That was Willie's idea, too, to put twice as much wire onto the second nail. That way, if more wire makes a stronger magnet, maybe the blue magnet would be twice as strong.

We started winding wire onto one of the nails.

We kept the wire pulled really tight. It was harder than I thought it would be. And if I'd had to do it all by myself, it would have been really boring.

By lunchtime we had only finished the nail with the red wire, the short wire.

For lunch we had chicken noodle soup and grilled cheese sandwiches. Dad made lunch because Mom and Abby were at the mall taking some clothes back. Gram had given Abby a sweater that went all the way down to her knees. It made her look like a Munchkin.

Dad said, "It's been pretty quiet up there. How's it going?"

Willie said, "We've been winding wire around a nail."

Dad said, "If it's taking too long, you could bring your things down to the workshop. I bet I could figure out how to make the nail spin around. That way, you could just hold the spool of wire and it would almost wind itself. Sound good?"

Willie started to nod his head, but I said, "That sounds great, Dad, but we'd better do the second nail like we did the first one. They should look the same way."

I felt a little sorry for my dad. He really wanted to help. It was hard for him to keep out of the way.

Then I said, "But when we're done winding the second nail, would you look at them for us?"

Dad said, "You bet. Just give a holler when you need me."

And I could tell it made my dad feel good to be invited.

When Willie and I finished winding the wire, we looked in one of the books to see how to hook the batteries together. And that's when I called my dad. Because if you hook big batteries together wrong, it can start a fire. And it said in the rules that if anything might be dangerous, ". . . an adult should be present."

Dad was great. He didn't try to change anything we were doing. He didn't say we should wind the wire some other way. And instead of being a K-I-A/D-I-A and telling us how to hook up the batteries, he made us think about it. Then we had to tell him how we wanted to do it.

We told him, and Dad said, "That's exactly right. You guys have got it all figured out." And then he left. Mom would have been proud of him.

Willie and I decided our first trial should be with just one battery. So we hooked the wire from each end of the red magnet onto the battery—one wire to the positive terminal and the other to the negative terminal.

But we didn't have anything to lift with the magnet. So we unhooked the wires and went downstairs and into the kitchen.

I said, "We need something that's made of iron or steel."

And Willie said, "And we have to know how much it weighs. Because it said in the science fair booklet to measure everything. So we have to measure the weight of what we pick up."

I opened the door to the basement, but Willie said, "Wait a minute."

Willie's been to my house so many times, he knows where everything is. He opened the pantry, and right away I knew what he was doing. He was going to get some cookies. But instead he grabbed a can off a shelf and said, "Tuna!"

"Tuna?" I said.

"Yeah," said Willie. "Tuna. This can of tuna weighs one hundred and seventy grams. And this can of soup weighs three hundred and five grams. And the cans are made of steel! Here, take some."

So I grabbed eight cans of soup, and he grabbed four cans of tuna.

If I told you every step of our experiment, it would make you crazy. About how we tried two batteries on the red magnet. And then tried to see if we could pick up a can of soup with the flat end of the nail. And how we used duct tape to stack two cans on top of each other so we could try to pick up two cans. And how we hooked the two batteries up to the blue magnet and then tried to lift soup again. And how we wrote down everything we tried. And then how we hooked up all four batteries and . . . but like I said, if I just told it all, you'd go nuts. Because me telling it wouldn't be as fun as really doing all this stuff with Willie, and he was cracking jokes and making faces, and coming up with all these good ideas.

It was a great afternoon. And when Willie's

dad showed up to take him home, our science fair experiment was practically finished. I mean, we still had a ton of work to do. And posters to make. And conclusions to write.

But Willie and I knew what we knew, and we knew why we knew it.

And the best part? The best part was that all afternoon, I didn't think about Kevin or Marsha or Mr. Lenny Cordo or his Bluntium Twelve computer system. Not once. It had been an afternoon of pure fun.

Which is what science is supposed to be in the first place, right?

Right.

CHAPTER ELEVEN

Winners

Then came the weekend before the science fair. Willie and I spent all Saturday and Sunday finishing our posters. We planned what we would say to the judges. We planned how to explain our conclusion.

We also had to be ready to explain our method. That's the part where we tested our idea. Judges can ask any questions they want about any part of the project. So you know what you have to be? You have to be a know-it-all, at least about your own project. Unless you have a good partner like Willie. Then you can be a know-about-half.

Willie and I were ready. We even remembered to buy four new batteries so the magnets would work just right.

On the Tuesday of the science fair, we brought our project to the school gym at five o'clock in the afternoon. That was part of the rules. We had an hour and a half to get everything ready. Then the judging would start at six thirty.

The gym was like a pot of water on a stove. The whole place felt like it was humming and bubbling, getting ready to boil over.

Kids were everywhere. And so were parents. Both my dad and Willie's dad came along to help us hang up our posters. Willie's dad had gone to an office store for us. He got one of those tall cardboard fold-up things. It was just the right size to hold our three posters.

There were numbered tables in rows up and down the floor, and there was a list of names by the door. Next to every name there was a number, and ours was forty-five.

Table number forty-five was a good one, right along the back wall. Except that it was next to table number forty-six. And table number forty-six was Kevin Young's table.

It was hard not to look at Kevin's stuff. He had three posters, just like ours. Except his didn't look like ours.

We had used markers to write the biggest words on our posters. We had used colored pencils and crayons to make our drawings. We had written out our words by hand.

Not Kevin. All the writing on his posters had been printed out from a computer. And so had his pictures. All the papers and letters and pictures had been glued onto Kevin's posters.

We had glued some things onto our posters, too. We had some drawings, and a great picture of a junkyard electromagnet holding up a crushed car. It's hard to glue stuff right, so some of our pictures had some little bumps and ridges in them. And so did our writing papers.

Not Kevin's. I don't know how he did it, but every picture and all his writing was glued down perfectly flat.

My dad looked at Kevin's posters. He nodded at Kevin's dad and said, "Great posters."

Kevin's dad looked a lot like Kevin. He had the same red hair and blue eyes. He smiled at my dad and said, "Thanks. We worked pretty hard on them."

See that? How Kevin's dad said "we"? I looked around at the other projects near us. And most of them looked like grown-ups had helped, too. It didn't seem very fair. All of a sudden I wished that I had let my dad help us. Because deep down, I still thought it would be nice to win that Bluntium Twelve computer.

Kevin looked over at our stuff once or twice. And I thought I saw him smile a little, but it wasn't a nice smile. It was a put-down smile.

But we had too much to do to think about Kevin for very long. We got our magnets wired up. We got our cans of soup and tuna stacked up. We laid out our notebooks and our method records.

And when everything was set up, we had forty minutes left over, so our dads took us out for hamburgers and chocolate shakes. The food was good, but Willie and I were pretty nervous.

At six thirty, the judges started. There were six of them, science and math teachers from the junior high school. First, they all just walked together up and down the rows of tables. Then they started at table number seventy-two, the last table. And we had to wait. And wait. And wait.

It took a long time for the judges to get to our row. Then it was another ten minutes before they got to Kevin at table forty-six.

It was good to hear the judges ask questions before it was our turn. And Kevin was good at answering them. He really was. He had done this experiment making ants learn how to go through a maze. He wanted to show that if ants can't smell, they get lost.

Ants leave something like an odor where they walk. And if one ant goes through the maze, it leaves a trail so others can follow. So after one ant went through the maze, Kevin let another one go, and it followed the same path. Then he painted the maze with lemon juice, let it dry, and let another ant go. The second ant got lost, so Kevin proved his hypothesis was right.

It was a good project. Even if Kevin did get help from his dad.

Then it was our turn. This lady judge started. She asked Willie to explain what we wanted to prove. Willie pointed at our posters and told how electromagnets work, and how we wanted to see what made the bigger difference, more wire or more power. He was great. Willie smiled, and he sounded like he was having fun. Because he was. And I could tell the judges liked that.

Then it was my turn. I had to explain our method. I took it slow, step by step. And while I talked, Willie hooked up the red magnet to two batteries and lifted up two cans of tuna. Then he added two more batteries and picked up four cans.

Then Willie took over talking. I hooked up two batteries to the blue magnet, the one that had more wire on it. And with two batteries, the blue magnet would pick up four cans! And with four batteries, it picked up eight cans of tuna.

I could tell that the judges liked what we were doing. Our results were different from what we had thought they would be, but we explained it all in our conclusion just right. We used the scientific method. It was a good experiment.

Kevin was watching, too. But I couldn't tell what he was thinking. He didn't smile or frown. And he hardly even blinked.

Then it was over. And it felt great. I looked at Willie, and he had that smile on his face, the really big one. And right then, I knew I didn't care if we won anything or not.

The judges moved on. Then it was time for more waiting, a lot more waiting. So Willie and I went to look around.

There was a lot of neat stuff to see. There were projects about cameras, about fruit, earthworms, carbon dioxide from plants, fruit flies, fossils, hot air balloons, soap bubbles, different kinds of sand, and a really great one on electric guitar sounds. And tons more.

We found Marsha's table, but we didn't go over. That's because she looked sad, and kind of mad, too, like she might start crying or yelling or something. Her posters looked great. There was this upside-down cake pan inside a box with a window cut in one side. The pan was hanging above a little lightbulb. I could tell from the posters that the pan had some grass growing from it.

Willie said, "What's wrong with her?"

I shrugged and didn't say anything. But I thought I knew why. Maybe it was because if you always feel like you have to be the best, it's hard. Because a lot of the time, someone else does just as well or even better.

Anyway, we kept walking. We looked at all the third-grade projects. And after I saw them all, I knew which one was going to win. There wasn't any question about it.

About a half hour later, it was time for the announcements. Everyone went into the auditorium. Willie and I sat in the tenth row, and our dads sat behind us. Mr. Lenny Cordo was there, and all the computer boxes were stacked up on the stage. It was pretty exciting.

The judges announced the fifth-grade winners first. Ellen Stone won the grand prize. She'd done the project about the electric guitar sounds. And second place went to Mark Nixon for a project about temperature and soap bubbles.

The fourth-grade winner was Charles LeClerc.

He had studied the hardness of different kinds of rocks. And second place went to Amy Martin's project about veins in leaves.

Then it was time for the third grade. My dad put his hand on my shoulder and gave a little squeeze. And the winner was . . . Pete Morris. Just like I knew it would be.

Pete had done this project about insect eggs and how different daylight hours make the eggs hatch. He had found some praying mantis eggs. He'd put some lights on a timer and had made the eggs hatch two months early. It was like he'd tricked them with the light. And there was this big glass box with about twenty baby praying mantises walking around on their little green legs.

The great thing was that Pete had started his project back in October. That was almost three months before Mrs. Karp announced the science fair. He wasn't doing the project to try to be better or smarter than anyone else. And he didn't do it to try to win a new computer. He did it because he really wanted to figure something out. Like I said, Pete's a science kid.

Willie and I were standing up clapping for

Pete. Then the head judge said, "And second prize in third grade goes to Phil Willis and Jake Drake for their project on electromagnets."

Then they called all of us up onto the stage, and we had to shake hands with the judges, and then with Mrs. Karp and Mr. Lenny Cordo. And Willie and I each got a little silver trophy that said:

SECOND PLACE
FIRST ANNUAL
DESPRES ELEMENTARY SCHOOL
SCIENCE FAIR

It was the best thing I ever won. And it wouldn't have been half as fun without Willie there, smiling his biggest smile at me.

We went back to the gym to take our project apart. Kevin and his dad were there at table forty-six. His dad looked kind of mad.

But Kevin didn't. He said, "Nice trophy."

I said, "Thanks. I thought your project was really good."

Kevin said, "I guess. Too bad you didn't win first place."

I said, "Yeah."

But really, I didn't think it was too bad. I was happy with second place. And here's why.

You see, Pete's project was the best. He would have won no matter what. And second place? Maybe I could have won second place all by myself. But I don't think so. Willie did a lot to make the project better. Plus we had fun. Plus we did it all ourselves.

The best part about the science fair was that suddenly, it was all over. I didn't have to think about it anymore. I didn't have to keep track of all those papers and batteries and pieces of wire.

When we took everything apart, Willie kept the blue magnet, and I took the one with the red wire. Whenever I open my junk drawer now, there it is.

But the trophy is on my shelf. I keep it there to remind myself that there's one thing I never want to be again. Ever. And that's Jake Drake, Know-It-All.

Jake Drake

CLASS CLOWN

For Priscilla Avery, the best neighbor
a first-year teacher ever had.
—A. C.

Contents

CHAPTER ONE   New Boss   1

CHAPTER TWO   Scared Stiff   9

CHAPTER THREE   Scared Silly   16

CHAPTER FOUR   Secret Information   24

CHAPTER FIVE   Unstoppable   30

CHAPTER SIX   Mr. Funny Bone   38

CHAPTER SEVEN   Christmas in April   48

CHAPTER EIGHT   Judge Brattle   57

CHAPTER NINE   No More Clowning   62

CHAPTER ONE

New Boss

I'm Jake, Jake Drake. I'm only ten years old, but I already have a full-time job. Because that's sort of how I think about school. It's my job.

I'm in fourth grade now, so I've had the same job for more than five years. And if you do something long enough, you get pretty good at it. That's how come I'm starting to be an expert about school.

I've had a bunch of different bosses so far. Because that's what a teacher is: the boss. And one thing I know for sure is that it's no fun when your boss is a sourpuss.

So far things have been okay for me. A few of my teachers have gotten grumpy now and then, and a couple of them have really yelled once in a while. And this year my fourth-grade teacher is Mr. Thompson, who can get grouchy sometimes. Plus he has brown hair growing out of his ears. So he might be a werewolf.

Still, I've never had a real sourpuss for a teacher—at least not for a whole school year.

But not Willie. Willie's my best friend, and last year his third-grade teacher was Mrs. Frule. She's one of those bosses who walks around with this mad look on her face, sort of like a cat when it's outside in the rain. If you go past her room, you feel like you should whisper and walk on tiptoe. Because if Mrs. Frule even looks at you, she can always find something to get mad about.

So third grade was tough for Willie because he's the kind of kid who loves to smile. Putting Mrs. Frule and Willie into the same classroom was a bad idea.

When I met Willie at lunch on our first day of third grade, I could tell something was wrong. He looked sort of pale, like maybe he was going to keel over or something. I said, "Hey, are you okay?"

And he said, "No, I'm *not* okay. Mrs. Frule already hates me. I spent half the morning getting yelled at, and the other half trying to figure out what I was doing wrong."

I asked, "What happened?"

Willie shrugged. "That's what I don't get. I didn't *do* anything. I was just sitting there, and all of a sudden I saw Mrs. Frule looking at me. So I smiled at her, and she frowned and said, 'Young man, wipe that smile off your face.' So I did. I wiped my hand across my mouth like this, and I stopped smiling. But that made Robbie Kenson start laughing, so then Mrs. Frule got real mad and she made me get up and walk out into the hall. And then she came out and leaned down, like, right into my face. She got so close I could see all the way up her nose. And she shook her finger at me and said, 'If you ever act like a smart aleck in my classroom again, you are going to be very, very sorry!'"

Poor guy. That was only Willie's first day of third grade, and it didn't get any better. All year long Mrs. Frule yelled at Willie at least three times a week. And he's one of the *good* kids! The kids like Jay Karnes and Zack Walton—real troublemakers? For those guys, being in Mrs. Frule's class was sort of like being in a prison camp. Maybe worse, because in a prison camp, if you mess up, you don't have to get a note signed by your parents.

My third-grade teacher was Mrs. Snavin, and she was pretty nice most of the time. I wished Willie could have switched to my class. But it doesn't work that way. Once school starts, you're stuck with your teacher for the whole year, and you just have to make the best of it.

And that's what Willie did. He didn't have a lot of fun in third grade, but he lived through it. Even Jay and Zack survived. Because that's what you do when your teacher is a grumphead. You learn what you have to do to stay alive, and you do it. And you know that once the year is over, you'll never have that boss again. So you just do your best and wait for summer.

Like I said, most of my teachers have been pretty nice. Actually, the grumpiest teacher I've had so far wasn't even a teacher. She was a student teacher. And I didn't have her for that long. Only about three weeks. Which was plenty. Her name was Miss Bruce.

Miss Bruce showed up on a Monday morning in April near the end of second grade. Mrs. Brattle was my regular teacher that year, and she said, "This is Miss Bruce. She's in college, and she's studying to be a teacher. As part of her college work, she's going to be here in our classroom for a while."

I looked at Miss Bruce. She was younger than Mrs. Brattle. A lot younger. She was so young that she sort of looked like Link Baxter's big sister. Except Link's sister was only in high school. Plus part of her hair was colored pink. Or sometimes purple.

Miss Bruce's hair was reddish blond. That first day she had on a blue shirt and a green skirt and blue shoes. Her nose was kind of small. Or maybe her nose was mostly hidden, because she wore a big pair of glasses with black rims. And her nose had freckles, too.

For her first three days Miss Bruce didn't do much. Sometimes she helped Mrs. Brattle pass

out papers. Once she read part of a story out loud. But most of the time she just sat in a chair near the back of the room and watched.

By Wednesday we'd gotten used to her hanging around. No one paid much attention to Miss Bruce. Except me. I kept looking at her during those first three days.

And I noticed something.

Back in second grade, Willie and I were both in Mrs. Brattle's class, so at lunch on Wednesday I asked Willie a question. I asked, "Have you noticed anything funny about Miss Bruce?"

"Funny?" said Willie. "You mean like the way she squints and wrinkles her nose when she looks at the chalkboard? I think that's kind of funny, don't you?"

"No," I said, "I mean funny like strange. Have you ever seen her smile?"

Willie was scraping the icing off an Oreo with his front teeth. He stopped right in the middle of the cookie. His eyes opened wide and he said, "You're right! I haven't seen her smile at all! Have you?"

I shook my head. "Nope. Not once. I wonder why."

Willie finished his first scrape and then started licking the leftovers. He stopped with his tongue sticking out. Then he gulped real fast and said, "Hey! Maybe she *can't* smile! Maybe she has a special problem, like if she smiles, her teeth fall out or something! Or maybe . . . maybe she's . . . an *alien!* Yeah, she's an alien, and she doesn't know how to smile, and . . . and she's going to use her special powers . . . to turn all of us into hamburgers and beam us up to her spaceship!"

Willie's like that. He has a lot of imagination.

But in a way, Willie was right. Miss Bruce *did* seem to have some special powers.

And there was one power she had that was going to change my life for a while. Because Miss Bruce was about to turn me into Jake Drake, Class Clown.

CHAPTER TWO

Scared Stiff

Thursday morning Mrs. Brattle asked us all to be quiet and listen. She asked Miss Bruce to come and stand next to her at the front of the classroom. Then Mrs. Brattle said, "For the next several weeks, Miss Bruce is going to be your teacher. I'm going to be helping Mrs. Reed in the library during this time, so I'll probably see you every day. And I'll even be here in the classroom sometimes. But Miss Bruce will be your teacher. I want all of you to be on your very best behavior for her."

And then Mrs. Brattle picked up her purse and a stack of papers and walked out of the room.

We all sat at our tables and looked at Miss Bruce. And Miss Bruce stood there at the front of the room and looked at us. Then she said, "Let's begin by talking about the rules." Her voice sounded kind of high and squeaky. "First of all, it is going to be quiet in my classroom. No talking, no whispering, and no shouting or laughing. You may not talk unless you raise your hand first and I give you permission. We have a lot of work to do, and we don't have time for any fooling around. I have very high expectations for each one of you, and I'm going to demand excellence. Is that clear?"

Miss Bruce lifted up her eyebrows, all the way above her big glasses. And she looked around the class. And she didn't smile.

I looked around too and I could see this look on everyone's face. Sort of a scared look. Even Link Baxter looked scared, and that almost never happened.

Then Miss Bruce clapped her hands together twice and said, "All right. Now. Let's not waste any time. Please get out your math workbooks."

Laura Pell raised her hand. When Miss Bruce nodded at her, Laura said, "We always have reading before math."

Miss Bruce didn't smile. She said, "What's your name?"

"Laura."

Miss Bruce said, "Laura, I want you to answer a question for me, all right?"

In a real small voice Laura said, "Okay."

"Now, Laura," said Miss Bruce, "who is your teacher?"

Laura smiled, because that was an easy question. She said, "My teacher is Mrs. Brattle."

Miss Bruce raised her eyebrows and leaned forward, and she said, "Now, Laura, please think. What did Mrs. Brattle just say? Who is your teacher for the next few weeks?"

In a tiny little voice Laura said, "You are."

Miss Bruce nodded at her and said, "That's right, Laura, *I* am your teacher now. And what did I ask you to do a minute ago?"

Laura said, "You said to get out our math workbooks."

Miss Bruce nodded. "And now I'm going to say it again: Class, please get out your math workbooks."

So we did. We all got out our math workbooks. Then we turned to page 47 like Miss Bruce told us to, and we did some addition problems. There was no talking. There was no whispering. There was no looking out the window. And there was no smiling.

We took the worksheet out of the workbook when Miss Bruce told us to. We wrote our names on our papers when Miss Bruce told us to. Then we passed in the papers. Quietly.

Then it was time for social studies. We had to read three pages in our *People and Places* book. Quietly. And then answer some questions on page 83. We had to write down our answers with no talking and no looking at our neighbors' papers. That's what Miss Bruce said. Like she thought we might cheat. And she didn't smile.

I looked over at Laura Pell. Her face didn't move, sort of like she was wearing a mask. She sat up straight in her chair. She didn't smile at all. She kept her eyes looking down at her table.

When she was done with her work, she folded her hands and put them in her lap. She looked like a statue.

And I knew why Laura was acting that way. She was scared of making a mistake. She was scared of Miss Bruce—scared stiff. Because when you get a grumphead for a boss, that can happen. And if your boss is grumpy and fussy and picky all at once, it's extra scary.

It was so quiet in our classroom. All I could hear was the squeaking of Miss Bruce's blue shoes as she walked around the room.

I took a quick look at the rest of the kids. Willie was scared. And Andrea Selton. Everyone was scared stiff, even Ben Grumson, who was even tougher to scare than Link Baxter.

And so was I. I sat still. Willie was sitting at my table, just two feet away, but I never looked at him. Because I was afraid we might smile at each other and get caught. And then Miss Bruce might get mad at us.

A part of me had decided to be careful. Part of me wanted to make sure there wasn't any trouble.

But there was another part of me that didn't

want to sit there like a bag of potatoes. This other part of me didn't want to just fold my hands and look down at my desk.

There was a part of me that didn't care if Miss Bruce got mad. That was the part of me that wanted to stand on my head and stick out my tongue and yell, really loud.

But did I?

No. That first day when Miss Bruce took over our class, I didn't dare.

I was too scared, just like everyone else.

CHAPTER THREE

Scared Silly

I'm usually happy on Friday mornings.

Friday means that the next day is Saturday, and on most Saturdays Willie and I mess around together. We watch some TV. We ride our bikes, play some computer games, and mostly have fun. If the weather's good, we work on our fort in the woods behind Willie's house. So Friday means work is almost over for the week.

But the Friday after Miss Bruce took over, I didn't feel happy. It felt like it was going to be the hardest day of my life.

On the bus ride to school that day, I thought, *Maybe Miss Bruce will be nicer today. Maybe she'll smile a little. Today will probably be a lot better than yesterday.*

I was wrong.

Friday started off like Thursday had. First we did a math worksheet. Instead of passing them in, we exchanged papers. Miss Bruce read the right answers for us. And she never smiled.

Then we did a map-skills sheet for social studies. We marked North, South, East, and West. We colored the rivers and lakes blue. We found the railroads and the highways. We found the mountains and the cities. Then Miss Bruce turned on the overhead projector and showed us how our maps should look. She said we could fix our maps if we had any mess-ups. That was sort of nice of her, but she never smiled.

Gym was great. Not because I love gym, because most of the time I don't. Gym was great because Miss Bruce wasn't there.

After gym, we all went back to class. There was no laughing, and nobody was late, not even one second.

Then Miss Bruce said we were going to have a spelling bee, and everyone was glad. Spelling bees are always fun, right? Wrong. Not when Miss Bruce is the boss.

Miss Bruce looked down at the seating chart and then looked through her big glasses at Meaghan Wright. She said, "You'll be first, Meaghan. Remember the rules: You have to say the word, then spell it, and then say it again. Ready?"

Meaghan nodded, so Miss Bruce said, "The first word is 'mouse.'"

Meaghan looked up at the ceiling. Then she took a deep breath and said, "M-o- . . ."

Miss Bruce shook her head and said, "Please stop."

Real fast, Meaghan said, "Oh, oh—I know. I forgot to say the word first, right? Mouse; m-o- . . ."

Shaking her head, Miss Bruce said, "I'm sorry, Meaghan, but you didn't follow the rules, and it's important that we all learn to follow directions exactly. So that means you are *out*."

Meaghan said, "But sometimes we get to have a second chance. Because I know how to spell the word."

Miss Bruce didn't smile. She didn't even blink. She shook her head and said, "I believe it's very important to be thinking all the time. That's what I expect of myself, and I expect it of every one of you, too. I'm sorry, but you are *out*."

Miss Bruce looked down at the seating chart, but I kept looking at Meaghan. I felt bad for her. She was chewing on her bottom lip. She looked like she might even cry.

Miss Bruce looked up from the chart. She looked right at Willie and said, "Philip, the word is 'mouse.'"

Willie smiled and said, "Um, Miss Bruce? Everyone calls me Willie, 'cause my last name is Willis. And I like Willie better than Philip too. So you can call me Willie."

Miss Bruce looked at Willie and said, "When we get to know each other a little better, then perhaps I'll use your nickname. But for now, I'd like to use your real name, all right? Now, Philip, the first word is *'mouse.'*"

For a second Willie looked like he thought Miss Bruce was kidding about calling him Philip. But she just stood there with her eyebrows up, waiting. Then he knew it was for real.

Willie was so surprised he didn't know what to do. So he gulped once or twice. And then he gulped some more.

Miss Bruce said, "I guess Philip is not ready to play, so for this round Philip is *out*." She looked down at the seating chart again, and then she looked right at me. "Jake, the first word is *'mouse.'*"

Maybe it was the look on Meaghan's face. Maybe it was the way Willie sat there gulping. Or maybe it was the way Miss Bruce kept saying *"out."* I don't know what it was, but something inside my head snapped.

I looked right at Miss Bruce and in a high, squeaky voice I said, "Mouse: m-i-c-k-e-y; mouse."

It took a second before everyone figured out what I had spelled. Then it sounded like every kid in the room took a deep breath. And held it.

Miss Bruce stared at me through her big glasses. "That was *not* the right word!"

So I kept using my best Mickey Mouse voice, and I said, "Heh, heh—well then, I guess I'm *out*."

I also guessed I was in trouble. But part of me didn't care.

Miss Bruce's face turned bright red. The paper in her hands started to shake. She looked like a cat when it's about to pounce.

Then Miss Bruce took three steps toward my chair. She frowned and said, "Jake, that was *not* funny!"

I took a quick look around the room. Everyone was grinning. And Willie was about to explode.

Miss Bruce was wrong. It *was* funny. Very funny.

Did Miss Bruce start yelling at me? Did she tell me to march down to the principal's office? Did she say, "I'll see *you* after school, Jake Drake!"

No.

Miss Bruce looked down at the seating chart. She kept looking at it for about five seconds—the longest five seconds of my life. And all that time I kept watching her face.

Then Miss Bruce looked up and said, "Annie, the word is still *'mouse.'* Spell it, please—*correctly.*"

And after Annie spelled it, Miss Bruce just

went on with the spelling bee. *She acted like nothing had happened!*

But something had happened—actually, two things had happened:

The first thing was, I had done something silly in front of the whole class. Everybody had almost laughed out loud—they thought I was really funny! That had never happened before, and I kind of liked it. Plus, I hadn't gotten in trouble. Amazing!

The second thing that happened was more like a mystery. Because I wasn't really sure it had happened. It had happened—that is, *maybe* it had happened—when Miss Bruce was looking down at her seating chart, when I was watching her face. And here's the mystery: I thought I saw something.

Something I'd never seen before.

There on Miss Bruce's face. Just for a second.

And it had looked sort of like . . . a *smile*.

CHAPTER FOUR

Secret Information

By the time we had library period on Monday, I was sure I'd made a mistake about what I saw on Friday. Miss Bruce smiling? Even a tiny little smile? No way.

All Monday morning we worked so hard. Miss Bruce pushed and pushed at us, every second. Math sheets, map skills, reading books, spelling drills. Even morning recess wasn't fun because we knew there was more work waiting for us. More work and no smiles.

But right before lunch we went to the library. Library period was great. A whole hour and tons of books. And no Miss Bruce. I mean, she was there, but she had to leave us alone for a while.

When we got there, I waved at Mrs. Brattle because she was helping in the library. She smiled and waved back.

Then I went to look for my Robin Hood book.

Robin Hood was my favorite book back when I was in second grade. I had never checked it out, because then I probably would have finished reading it in two days. I only read it during library period. That way, it lasted longer. Like a good jawbreaker.

I knew right where to look, and the book was there.

All the soft chairs were filled up. Plus it was sort of noisy at the front of the media center. So I took my book to the back of the big room, where it was quiet.

I sat on the carpet between some shelves. I leaned against the wall. Then I opened the book, and there I was: Me and Robin Hood and Little John, riding our horses through Sherwood Forest.

I was really into the story when I heard someone say, "I have to talk with you." And the voice wasn't in my book. It was in the library.

And I knew that voice. It was Miss Bruce.

And I thought, *Great. I'm at the best part of my book, and she has to talk with me.*

I started to stand up. Then another voice said, "All right, Hannah. We can talk right here."

And I knew that voice too. It was Mrs. Brattle. On the other side of the bookshelves. Three feet away.

I guess I could have made a noise. Or I could have stood up and started to look at the books on the shelf so they would see me.

But I didn't. I thought maybe I'd get in trouble for being way in the back of the library. Maybe they'd both yell at me.

So I froze. I just sat there.

I tried not to listen. I even put my hands over my ears. But I heard them anyway.

Mrs. Brattle said, "Sorry I didn't have time to talk with you on Friday afternoon. How's everything going?"

Miss Bruce said, "Well, something happened right before lunch on Friday . . . and I'm not sure what to do about it."

"Oh?" said Mrs. Brattle. "What happened?"

And what did Miss Bruce talk about? She talked about me. She told Mrs. Brattle all about my big joke during the spelling bee.

And sitting there, I couldn't believe my ears. You know how you can tell a lot from hearing someone's voice? Well, even without seeing her, I could tell Miss Bruce was smiling. Smiling!

She even giggled a little and said, "I wish you could have seen Jake's face. He was *so* funny! He's such a cutie. I almost cracked up!"

Mrs. Brattle said, "Well, it's a good thing you didn't. Once you start laughing along with the kids, things can get out of hand very quickly."

"That's what my college teacher said too," said Miss Bruce. "She told us that the rule is, 'Don't smile until Christmas.'"

Mrs. Brattle chuckled and said, "Yes, I learned that too, and it's a good rule, especially when you're just starting out. Or when you're a substitute. Sometimes all it takes is one smile, and the kids will think they can get away with anything."

It was quiet for a few seconds. Then Miss

Bruce said, "What do you think? Should I do something about Jake?"

"Jake?" said Mrs. Brattle. "Don't worry. He's a good boy. Still, you'll have to keep your eye on him. But if that's your biggest problem, then it sounds like you're doing just fine. Now, we'd better get back up front to the kids. It's getting a little too loud up there."

Then their voices got softer as they walked away.

I sat there on the floor. My heart was pounding. My mouth was dry.

I crawled forward and peeked around the corner of the shelf. When no one was looking, I slipped out and moved to a different part of the library.

I felt like a second-grade spy. And now I had some secret information: Miss Bruce wasn't an alien. She knew how to smile. And giggle.

Plus, she thought I was a cutie.

And best of all, she thought I was *funny*.

When you're only eight years old, and you get this kind of secret information, it can start something.

And that something is called trouble.

CHAPTER FIVE

Unstoppable

All during lunch on Monday, I wanted to tell Willie. I wanted to tell him that Miss Bruce was a giggler. And that I was a cutie.

But I didn't. Because the best part of a secret is the part that makes it a secret. And that's keeping it.

Back in our room after lunch recess, I wasn't sure what to do. So for a while I didn't do anything. Except more work. Because right after lunch we had silent reading.

Miss Bruce told us to read a story in our

reading books. Anyone who finished was supposed to read a second story. And anyone who
finished the second story was supposed to read
a third story. That way, the fast readers would
keep busy while the slow readers were finishing
the first story.

And then when everyone was done reading the
first story, we were going to talk about it.

I was a pretty fast reader back in second
grade, so I was almost done with the third story
when Miss Bruce clapped her hands twice and
said, "All right, class. Everyone please turn to
page seventy-seven in your reading book. Let's
begin by talking about *who* was in this story."
Miss Bruce looked down at the seating chart and
said, "Andrea, can you tell us the name of one
person who was in the story?"

And Andrea did. She said, "Jim."

Which wasn't so hard. There were only three
people in the whole story. And the story was only
twelve pages long. Plus it had lots of pictures.

Then Carlos told the next *who*, and Lisa told
the last *who*.

So we were done with the *who* part. Which

had been pretty boring. I thought Mrs. Brattle would have done it better.

But that's why Miss Bruce was there. So she could learn to be less boring. Someday. Maybe.

After the *who* came the *where*.

Miss Bruce said, "Now, tell the class *where* the story happened, Link."

Which was also super easy.

Except Link wasn't listening.

Link shoved something under the table and looked at Miss Bruce. And Link had that look in his eyes: the lost look.

Link said, "Um . . . where? Oh, yeah . . . where. Um . . . what was the question?"

Miss Bruce tilted her head and looked down at where Link had his hands under the table. Then her eyes got narrow and she pushed her lips together.

And I knew what was going to happen next. I could see it all: Miss Bruce was going to walk over and hold out her hand. Then she would say, "Link, give me that." And Link would pull out a comic book, or a toy, or something else really stupid. Then Miss Bruce would stare at him until

he was really scared. She would make Link feel bad about not paying attention. Just like she had done to Laura and Meaghan.

Back in second grade, Link wasn't very nice. Most of the time he was a bully. So it wasn't very often that I felt sorry for Link.

But I did. At that moment, I felt sorry for him. And I felt sort of mad at Miss Bruce. Because I felt like she was sort of being a bully too.

So before Miss Bruce had a chance to walk over to Link, I raised my hand and started waving it around.

Miss Bruce turned and looked at me.

She didn't want to call on me. I could tell she wasn't done with Link. I kept waving my hand in the air anyway.

So Miss Bruce said, "Yes, Jake?" She knew my name without looking at the seating chart.

I said, "I think I know where the story happened."

Miss Bruce wasn't sure what to do. She wanted to go after Link, but now she had called on me, and I had an answer. So she said, "Well, then . . . then tell us, Jake. Where?"

"Well . . . ," I said slowly, "I'm not *exactly* sure . . ."

She said quickly, "Then just tell us where you *think* the story happened, Jake." Miss Bruce wanted to finish with me and get back to Link.

I said, "So I should just tell you? Like right now?"

She nodded her head at me.

Even slower, I said, "Even if I'm not *completely* sure?"

Miss Bruce said, "Yes, Jake. Even if it's only a guess. *Where* do you think this story happened?"

I looked Miss Bruce right in the eye and I said, "Well, I . . . I *think* it happened . . . on Earth!"

I kept staring into Miss Bruce's eyes. I heard a girl behind me giggle. But I didn't smile. I tried not to blink. I just waited.

Every kid in the room knew I had made a joke. Miss Bruce knew it too. But I kept acting like I was serious.

If she still thought I was a cutie, Miss Bruce did a good job of not showing it. She pushed her lips together into a thin line and glared at me. Then she said, "Yes. That's true. Of *course* the story happened on Earth, Jake." No smile. Not even a hint.

She turned back to Link. And now Link had his hand up. Whatever he had been hiding under the desk was gone.

Miss Bruce nodded at him and Link said, "The story happened by the ocean, right?"

"Yes, Link," said Miss Bruce. Then she took a deep breath. I thought she was going to walk over to Link and get mad at him anyway. Or maybe she would turn and get mad at me.

But she didn't. She let out her deep breath. Then she looked down at her seating chart again. She said, "Now, Ted, can you tell me *what* happened in our story?"

Ted was having a hard time. The corners of his mouth were wiggling. He wanted to smile, but he knew he'd better not.

I looked around the room. Half the kids in the class were smiling, and the other half were trying not to, like Ted.

There was only one person in the whole room who wasn't having any fun. And that was Miss Bruce.

But I wasn't thinking about Miss Bruce, not right then. I was too busy. I was enjoying myself. Because for the second time in two days, I'd done something funny. And I'd gotten away with it both times!

I was the new class clown. I was unstoppable.

CHAPTER SIX

Mr. Funny Bone

When I got home from school on Monday afternoon, I asked my mom if I could have a snack. Because being so funny had made me hungry.

So Mom made me some peanut butter on crackers. Plus a glass of milk.

As I was eating I started to think. I tried to remember other times I had been funny at school. Like back when I was in first grade. Or kindergarten. I tried to remember. And I couldn't think of any.

And now, all of sudden, I had made everyone

want to start laughing—twice! And it had been so easy. I hadn't even been trying that hard.

I stopped right in the middle of drinking my milk. And I thought to myself, *If you're this funny without even trying, think how funny you could be if you worked at it!* I decided I could probably become the funniest kid in the history of the universe! And I could start the very next day!

If I was going to be super funny, I'd need super jokes. And I'd have to tell them just right.

So I went to find Abby. She's my little sister. When I was in second grade, Abby was in kindergarten. I found her in her room listening to a story cassette of *The Three Little Pigs.*

I went over to the cassette player and shut it off.

Abby said, "Hey! Put it back on!"

"Wait," I said, "because I want to try telling you some jokes. Okay?"

Abby crossed her arms and frowned. "I don't want jokes. I want the pigs."

"C'mon," I said. "It'll be fun. Are you ready?"

Abby scratched her knee. And made a face at

the ceiling. And sat up on the edge of her bed. Then she said, "Okay."

So I said, "Knock, knock."

Abby wrinkled her nose. She said, "What?"

"I said, 'Knock, knock.' You know—it's a knock-knock joke."

Abby shook her head. "That's not funny."

"That's 'cause the joke's not over yet. Listen," I said. "I say 'Knock, knock,' then you say 'Who's there?', okay?" Then I said, "Knock, knock."

And Abby said, "Who's there, okay?"

"No," I said. "You just say 'Who's there?' That's all you say. Just 'Who's there?' Now, let's try it again. Ready?"

Abby nodded her head.

So I said, "Knock, knock."

And Abby said, "Who's there?"

And I said, "Toodle."

And Abby laughed. She clapped her hands and said, "Toodle's funny. Tell another one."

"No, no," I said. "'Toodle' isn't the funny part. I say 'Knock, knock.' Then you say 'Who's there?' Then I say 'Toodle,' and then you say 'Toodle *who*?' and *then* I finish the joke."

Abby looked at me. She said, "Toodle *was* funny. I don't want more joke."

"C'mon," I said. "I have to finish it, okay? I'm going to start over again."

Abby frowned. "Don't want to."

But I said, "Knock, knock."

And Abby said, "Who's there, okay?"

"No!" I yelled. "You just say 'Who's there?' Get it right, Abby!"

Abby shook her head. And then she yelled, "Mommeeee! MOMMEEEE!" Abby can really yell.

Mom ran up the stairs and into Abby's room in about two seconds. "What's the matter—are you hurt?" Then Mom saw me. She said, "Oh! Jake. Good. You're here too. Is everyone all right? Why did you call me like that, Abby?"

Abby pointed at me. "Because of him. He won't stop making a joke."

Mom frowned at me. "Have you been teasing Abby again, Jake?"

"No!" I said. "I'm not teasing her. I'm just trying to tell one stupid little knock-knock joke. And she can't even do it. And it's driving me crazy!"

Mom said, "Well, why don't you tell me the knock-knock joke. Then Abby can listen and see how it works, all right?"

I said, "Okay. Knock, knock."

And Mom said, "Who's there?"

And I said, "Toodle."

And Mom said, "Toodle who?"

And I said, "Toodle-oo to you too!"

Mom smiled and nodded. She said, "That's a good one."

Abby shook her head. "No. Just toodle. Toodle was better."

And that's when I went to my room. To practice telling jokes by myself.

I stood in front of the mirror that's above my dresser. I looked at myself and I started telling jokes.

Knock, knock.
Who's there?
Seven, eight, nine.
Seven, eight, nine who?
Sven ate nine cookies!

Knock, knock.
Who's there?
Robins go.
Robins go who?
No! Robins go tweet; *owls* go who!

What goes "Ha ha bonk"?
A man who laughs his head off!

If I had five baseballs in one hand,
and I had five baseballs in the
other, what would I have?
Really BIG hands!

What's worse than finding a worm in
your apple?
Finding half a worm!

It's not much fun telling jokes to yourself, so I got tired of that pretty fast. But as I looked in the mirror, I remembered how great I am at making funny faces.

So I practiced crossing my eyes and sticking

my tongue out. I practiced pushing my nose up and making a pig face. I practiced puffing up my cheeks and pulling my eyelids out of shape. No doubt about it: I was a pretty funny kid.

But after a while my face got tired. And my eyes started to hurt from crossing them so much.

So I looked on my bookshelf until I found this book of jokes I got at a book fair. And I sat on my bed and I read the whole book. Then I lay down on my stomach and read it again. The whole book.

I guess being so funny had made me tired, because I fell asleep with my face in the joke book. And the next thing I knew, Mom was calling to me to come downstairs for dinner.

When I went into the kitchen, my dad smiled at me and said, "Hey, Jake! What's new?"

And I said, "The moon."

Dad said, "The moon?"

And I said, "Yup. There's a new moon every month."

Dad and Mom laughed, and Dad said, "That's a good one, Jake."

Abby said, "It's not as funny as toodle."

We all sat at the table and I looked at the food. Right away I said, "Hey, Mom, know what they make from lazy cows? Meatloaf! Get it? Loaf? Like lazy? I just made that up! Pretty funny, huh?"

Mom smiled and nodded as she passed the potatoes. "Yes, pretty funny, Jake."

Then I said, "Hey, Dad, know how come the farmer ran a steamroller across his fields?"

Dad smiled and shook his head. So I said, "Because he wanted to grow some mashed potatoes!"

Dad laughed and said, "Mashed potatoes! That's a good one!"

All during dinner the jokes just kept on coming. It was like anything I looked at turned into a joke. Sometimes I remembered jokes, and sometimes I made up new ones. I even made my fish face at Abby when she was drinking her milk. Which made a big mess. But that was funny too!

When we had dessert, I said, "Hey, Dad, do you use your right hand or your left hand when you eat ice cream?"

"I guess I use my right hand."

And I said, "That's funny—I always use a *spoon*!"

I was hilarious!

When I asked to be excused, Dad said, "You sure are Mr. Funny Bone tonight, Jake. How'd all this get started?"

And like a dope I said, "Oh, it started at school."

Wrong thing to say.

Right away Dad frowned. He said, "Well, I hope you're getting it all out of your system before tomorrow morning. Being funny like this at school isn't a good idea, Jake. You understand that, right?"

And I nodded and I said, "Oh, I know that." And that was true. Because I knew it wasn't a good idea.

No, being funny at school on Tuesday wasn't a *good* idea: It was a *great* idea!

CHAPTER SEVEN

Christmas in April

On Tuesday morning Miss Bruce piled on the work. All my practice being Mr. Funny Bone wasn't any help at all. We had so much to do that I didn't have a chance to tell a single joke.

Plus, Miss Bruce was acting grumpier and grumpier.

When we were doing some math work, Carlos got up and started walking to the back of the room.

Miss Bruce looked at him and said, "Carlos, please stay in your seat and keep working. Math time is almost over."

He held up his pencil. "Gotta sharpen this."

Miss Bruce said, "I'm sure it's fine for now. Please keep working."

Carlos said, "But my pencil has to be extra sharp when I do math. It helps me make good numbers."

Miss Bruce said, "What did I tell you to do, Carlos?"

Carlos said, "You told me to sit down. But I need my pencil sharper. Honest."

Miss Bruce said, "You're wasting time, Carlos, and you have to finish all your math problems. So sit. Get back to work. Now."

Carlos walked slowly back to his chair and sat down.

Right away Annie reached across the table and handed Carlos a pencil.

Miss Bruce looked at Annie and she said, "Annie! *What* are you doing?"

Annie froze. She couldn't speak.

Miss Bruce said, "Annie, answer me!"

So Annie sort of hunched her shoulders and said, "I had an extra pencil. A sharp one."

Miss Bruce frowned, and I thought she was

going to start yelling. But she said, "Fine. That was very nice of you, Annie. Now, get back to work, both of you. Because anyone who does not finish all the math problems will have to stay in during recess."

Miss Bruce was acting so grumpy that I kind of got scared again. It was like my dad had said: Trying to be funny at school didn't seem like a good idea. I wanted to tell some jokes, but I didn't want to run in front of a train. And at that moment Miss Bruce seemed a lot like a locomotive.

So I finished my math problems, and so did everyone else. Then Miss Bruce told us to take out our spelling workbooks. And we did. And then Miss Bruce told us to turn to page 62. And we did. And we got right to work.

The spelling work was easy. It's the kind of work that leaves plenty of room inside your head for other stuff. So I started thinking about how funny I had been at dinner the night before.

And sitting there copying over words that end with "tch," I remembered something I'd forgotten to practice at home. Something very funny. Something I'm great at: noises.

Like my mouth-pops. I can make this really loud POP by pulling my tongue off the roof of my mouth. It's a great noise.

And I also make a good duck sound. I can quack by pushing air out of one side of my mouth. Plus I can laugh sort of like Donald Duck.

But my best sound is the one I always practice when Willie and I have sleepovers. And that's burping. Willie's a pretty good burper too, but I'm a better burper.

To make a big burp, all you have to do is gulp some air down into your stomach. And then you let it come back out as a burp. Simple.

So I was sitting there on that Tuesday morning doing my spelling work. Plus thinking about burping.

I wrote *patch*. And then I took a gulp of air.

I wrote *catch*. And I took a gulp of air.

I wrote *latch*. And I took a gulp of air.

I wrote *pitch*. Another gulp of air.

I wrote *ditch*. And I took one more gulp of air.

It wasn't until I took that fifth gulp of air that I remembered something. I wasn't at a sleepover at Willie's house. I was at school.

I straightened up in my chair and leaned back a little. It felt like I had a balloon stuffed under my T-shirt. But it wasn't a balloon. It was my stomach. I tapped on it with my pencil. It made a hollow sound, sort of like a tom-tom.

And that's when Miss Bruce came right up behind me and said, "Are you all done with your work, Jake?"

I turned around real fast and looked up into her face. And I said, "Nope."

That's what I *tried* to say. But I *actually* said, "NOOOOOOOOOOOOOOOOOOOOOOOOOOOOPE."

It was the longest, loudest burp of my life!

The classroom was completely quiet. Everyone stared at me. Including Miss Bruce.

Don't ask me how I got the idea to do what I did next, because I don't know. There was Miss Bruce with her arms folded, looking down at me through her huge black glasses, and what did I do? I patted my chest, and I crossed my eyes, and I said, "Pardon me! It must have been that frog I ate for breakfast!"

Miss Bruce stood there. She was trying to get mad. She wanted to frown and yell and shake her finger at me and tell me that I had been terribly, terribly rude.

But she couldn't. I was just too funny. Plus I was a cutie.

So what did Miss Bruce do? She smiled! And it wasn't a little smile. It was a great big smile with teeth and everything. It was almost a grin. Every kid in the class saw that smile. And they also heard her giggle.

Miss Bruce's teacher at college had said, "Don't smile until Christmas." On that April morning, I was Santa Claus. Christmas had arrived!

After Miss Bruce smiled and giggled, everybody laughed a little. Then Miss Bruce covered her mouth with her hand and shook her head. And she tried to look serious again.

She said, "Let's not get silly, class. Please keep working on your spelling." And it almost worked. We all started to quiet down.

Then Willie burped almost as loud as I had and said, "I had *two* frogs for breakfast!"

All the kids laughed at that, much louder, and Susan Tuttle said, "Oooh! Gross!"

When a class starts laughing, it's sort of like when a volcano begins to rumble. Because it doesn't seem like much at first, but it's still dangerous.

Miss Bruce clapped her hands twice and said, "Class, that's enough!"

But the class didn't think it was enough. We were just getting started.

Link Baxter stood up and put his hands up under his arms and started hopping around the back of the room. "Hey, look! Look! I'm a frog. Ribbet! Ribbet!"

Miss Bruce clapped again. "Link, sit down! All of you, be quiet!"

No one was listening. Willie was still burping. Link was still hopping around the back of the room.

Then Ted tossed a ball of paper at Ben, and Ben threw it back to him. Carlos waved his arms and called, "Hey, Ted! Ted! Over here!"

And they started to play keep-away while Annie and Meaghan called out, "Yay, Ben! Yay, Carlos! Hey, toss it to us, too!"

Miss Bruce shouted, "QUIET!"

But it kept getting louder and louder and louder. Our room had turned into an erupting volcano of laughing and shouting and goofing around.

And once that kind of volcano gets going, there's usually only one thing that can stop it: a real teacher.

Except there is one other way to plug the volcano. I saw it happen that morning.

Because if a student teacher stamps her feet and screams, "Stop it! Stop it!" and then bursts out crying and runs out of the classroom and slams the door, the volcano shuts down. And the room gets quiet.

Very, very quiet.

CHAPTER EIGHT

Judge Brattle

Mrs. Brattle walked into the room two minutes after Miss Bruce had run out.

Twenty-three kids were doing spelling work.

Silently.

No one even looked up at Mrs. Brattle. No one dared.

Mrs. Brattle sat down at the front of the room. She tapped a pencil on her desk and said, "Please stop working."

When we were all looking at her, she said,

"Now, who will tell me what happened in here? With Miss Bruce."

Mrs. Brattle was wearing a white shirt and a black sweater. She looked like a lady judge on one of those TV shows. Judge Brattle. She tapped her pencil on her desk again and looked around the room. She said, "I'm waiting. . . ."

I wanted to stand up and say, "Your Honor, it was all my fault. I'm just too funny. And I knew that Miss Bruce was a secret giggler. And I didn't mean to burp, but after I did, I said that thing about the frog. And that's what got everything so crazy. And I'm sorry that I'm so hilarious."

But I didn't say that. I didn't say anything.

Instead, Marsha McCall raised her hand. And when Mrs. Brattle called on her, Marsha started talking. And she talked in questions like she always does. She said, "Well, we were working on our spelling lessons? Because you know how it's Tuesday? And you know Miss Bruce? How she started laughing after Jake burped? Well, you know how it's hard to stop laughing sometimes? Don't you think maybe that's what happened? That everybody couldn't stop laughing?"

Marsha said a lot of words, but Mrs. Brattle only heard three of them. Mrs. Brattle turned and looked at me. And she said, "'After Jake burped?' Did Marsha just say 'after Jake burped'? Tell me a little more about that part of the story, Jake."

So I said, "I didn't mean to. But I did. Burp. And it was a big burp too. And then I said something funny."

Mrs. Brattle raised her eyebrows. She said, "Something funny?"

I nodded. "Yeah. I guess it was funny. I said it must have been the frog I ate for breakfast."

The corners of Mrs. Brattle's mouth wiggled a little, but she didn't smile. She said, "I see. And then what happened?"

"It just started to get silly. In the room. After Miss Bruce smiled. Because she never smiled at all until then. Not even once. And then she laughed a little too. And then . . . it got loud. That's all."

I guess I could have told Mrs. Brattle how Ted and Ben had been throwing stuff and how the girls had been yelling and how Willie had kept burping and Link kept hopping around.

But I didn't. Because I knew none of that would have happened if I hadn't been so funny. It was all my fault.

I guess that's what Mrs. Brattle thought too. Because she stood up and said, "Class, Mrs. Reed is on her way here. While she's here, I want you to finish your spelling and then you may do some silent reading. *Silent* reading."

Then she turned and looked at me. She said, "Jake, stand up. You're coming with me."

As we walked out of the courtroom, Judge Brattle didn't smile.

And neither did I.

CHAPTER NINE

No More Clowning

I thought Judge Brattle was taking me to jail. Which would have been the principal's office.

So I was surprised when she marched right past the office. Instead, she stopped at a door marked TEACHERS' ROOM. She opened the door and said, "In here, Jake."

I'd never been in the teachers' room before. It was pretty nice in there. There was a big couch and a refrigerator. There was a little table in front of the couch with some magazines on it. One wall was covered with a huge bulletin board. Which was kind of messy. There was a big bookcase. There was even a Coke machine. Definitely the best room in the whole school.

And sitting at the big table in the middle of the room was Miss Bruce. With a box of tissues. And a red nose.

Miss Bruce's big glasses were next to the box of tissues. Without her glasses on, Miss Bruce looked like she was in high school. Just a girl with puffy eyes and a runny nose.

Mrs. Brattle pulled out a chair for me across from Miss Bruce. She walked around the table and sat down next to her student teacher.

Then Mrs. Brattle said, "Jake, is there something you want to say to Miss Bruce?"

I wanted to say, "Knock, knock." Because Miss Bruce looked like she needed a joke to cheer her up. But I knew that wasn't a good idea. So I said what Mrs. Brattle wanted me to. I said, "I'm sorry I was so funny in class. And I'm sorry I made you giggle. By being so funny."

Miss Bruce dabbed at her eyes and said, "It's

okay, Jake. I'm sorry I got so upset. I didn't want to. And I shouldn't have. But it's all over now. So it's okay."

Mrs. Brattle shook her head and said, "Actually, it's not okay, Miss Bruce. Jake shouldn't have been trying to do anything except be good and get his work done. Right, Jake?" I nodded. "And if you make a rude noise by mistake, then all you need to say is 'Excuse me.' Is that clear?" I nodded again. Mrs. Brattle narrowed her eyes and looked right into my face. "Jake, it *was* a mistake, right? When you burped?"

And I looked right back into Mrs. Brattle's eyes. And I was so glad that I could tell the truth, because Judge Brattle would have been able to tell I was lying. I said, "Yes. I didn't burp on purpose."

Mrs. Brattle nodded. "I'm glad to know that, at least. But the silliness has got to stop. Now. Do you understand?"

I nodded. "Uh-huh. No more silliness."

Mrs. Brattle said, "All right, then. Miss Bruce, is there anything else you want to say?"

Miss Bruce shook her head. She looked a lot

better. But I could still tell she had been crying. She said, "No. Nothing else."

Then Mrs. Brattle said, "Jake, how about you? Anything else?"

It was one of those times when I should have known to keep my mouth shut. I should have just shaken my head and sat there looking scared. Or maybe I should have whispered "No, thank you," and folded my hands in my lap. But I didn't.

I looked right at Miss Bruce and I said, "Miss Bruce, how come you never smiled until today? Was that because of what your teacher said? About Christmas?"

Oops. BIG oops! The second I said that I knew I had made a major goof.

Miss Bruce's eyes opened wide. And so did Mrs. Brattle's. They both looked at me. And then they looked at each other. And then back at me. Mrs. Brattle folded her arms.

And I knew they knew. They knew I had heard them talking that day in the library.

Miss Bruce sat up straight in her chair. Even without the big glasses, her eyes were plenty scary. She said, "Why . . . why you little *sneak*!

You were *spying* on me!" I was glad she was over on the other side of the big table.

I gulped and said real fast, "No, really, I wasn't spying! That day in the library? I didn't mean to hear you talking. I didn't do it on purpose. I was just sitting there reading *Robin Hood*, and you came to where I was, and I was afraid I'd get in trouble for sitting in the back, and then you started talking. You just started talking! I tried not to listen. But I heard you anyway. I didn't mean to. And I didn't tell anyone about it. Honest! And I'm sorry." I was looking back and forth between their faces.

I could tell they believed me. But I still felt like Miss Bruce was going to jump over the table and come after me.

Mrs. Brattle took charge. She said, "Seems like you have quite a lot to be sorry about today, Jake. But I think Miss Bruce and I understand the situation. And, if Miss Bruce will accept your apology, then so will I, and we'll just put all of this business behind us. All right, Miss Bruce?"

Miss Bruce nodded. But it wasn't a very big nod.

"Very well, then," said Mrs. Brattle, standing

up. "Then let's get you two back to class."

Miss Bruce kind of jumped a little in her chair. "Me?" she asked. "You mean I have to go back? To your class? Today?"

Mrs. Brattle looked down at Miss Bruce and smiled. "Why, of course you do. Right now. You're the teacher."

Miss Bruce looked like someone had just told her to go for a walk in a graveyard. At midnight. Without a flashlight. She was scared.

And then I got it: She was scared of *us*—of the kids! Of noise and silliness and craziness! Miss Bruce was scared, and Mrs. Brattle wasn't. Because Mrs. Brattle was a real teacher.

Miss Bruce bit her lip. She looked at Mrs. Brattle and said, "Don't you think you should come with me?"

Mrs. Brattle shook her head. "No, you'll be fine. The class will be waiting to see what happened to Jake, and Jake is going to look like he's had a good scolding. Jake is also going to be a perfect *angel* from this moment on. And *you* are going to walk back into that room and show all the boys and girls that just because you smile once in a while does not mean that they can go wild and misbehave."

Miss Bruce said, "But . . . but I *cried*. All those kids saw me cry and run out of the room! I *can't* go back."

Mrs. Brattle smiled and patted Miss Bruce on the arm. "Don't worry, dear. Everyone understands about crying, especially children. When it happens, you dry your face off, and then you go on with whatever you have to do. And *you* have a class to teach."

Then Mrs. Brattle took hold of the back of Miss Bruce's chair, so Miss Bruce had to stand up.

"There we go," said Mrs. Brattle. "Now, you and Jake run along. Mrs. Reed is needed back in the library. And Jake, from now on, I want nothing but good news about you, is that clear?"

I nodded.

And then Miss Bruce and I walked down the hall to our classroom.

I did what Mrs. Brattle said. I walked into the room. I sat down. I didn't look at anybody. I didn't smile. I tried to look like I had just lived through the worst ten minutes of my life. I tried to look like I was happy just to be alive.

And it turned out that Mrs. Brattle was right. Not one kid tried to be silly. Not one kid was noisy or rude.

And Miss Bruce did great. After all that yelling and the crying and the running out of the room, she acted like it wasn't a big deal. And because she acted that way, it wasn't. It was like none of it had ever happened.

But it had happened. And I had the proof. Because I kept on being funny.

Except I was never funny in class. And not when Miss Bruce was around. Or Mrs. Brattle.

So mostly I was funny for Willie. Before school, at recess, in gym class, on Saturdays— every chance I got, I told Willie jokes and made funny noises and faces at him. At lunch one day I made a pig face, and Willie laughed so hard he snorted a chunk of Oreo right out of his nose! I was a riot!

But after about three weeks, Willie was starting to go crazy, and I was starting to run out of jokes. So one day I just stopped. And I'm glad I did, because it's hard to try to be funny *all* the time. It's much better to save up silliness for special occasions. Like sleepovers. Or long bus rides.

The rest of Miss Bruce's student-teaching time went by pretty fast. And the best part is she wasn't as grumpy or as picky or as fussy as before. It was like Miss Bruce didn't have to be that way anymore. Because she wasn't afraid. I guess if you can laugh and giggle, and then watch your class go nuts, and then scream and yell, and then run out of the room crying, and *then* come back and have everything be okay, there's not much left to be scared about.

Mrs. Brattle planned a surprise party for Miss Bruce at the end of her three weeks. We all signed a big card we made for her in art class. And when Mrs. Brattle gave her a book and a hug, I thought Miss Bruce was going to start crying and run out of the room again.

But she didn't. She blinked a lot. And then she smiled. It was a big smile, with teeth and everything. Her voice sounded wobbly. And she said, "I learned so much here at Despres Elementary School. And I know that no matter how many other places I go and no matter how many other children I teach, I'm never going to forget you."

Miss Bruce was talking to the whole class. But at the end, she looked right at me. And I got this feeling that what she meant was, she was never going to forget me: Jake Drake, Class Clown.

Andrew Clements

has been hailed by the *New York Times* as "a proven master at depicting the quirky details of grade school life." His many celebrated books include the contemporary classic *Frindle* and the *New York Times* bestsellers *The Landry News* and *The Report Card*. He and his wife, the parents of four grown children, live in Westborough, Massachusetts.